OLIVIA

JOHN HUNT

Black Rose Writing | Texas

ISBN: 978-1-68513-047-3
PUBLISHED BY BLACK ROSE WRITING
www.blackrosewriting.com

Printed in the United States of America
Suggested Retail Price (SRP) $19.95

Olivia is printed in Garamond

*As a planet-friendly publisher, Black Rose Writing does its best to eliminate unnecessary waste to reduce paper usage and energy costs, while never compromising the reading experience. As a result, the final word count vs. page count may not meet common expectations.

This book is dedicated to my mother, Catherine Hunt
You fought long and hard. Rest well, mom, you earned it.
We miss you.

SPECIAL THANKS

Thank you, Dallas Baker and Ethan Hunt. You were brutal with your edits and suggestions. And as such, you made this book better.

Thank you to Detective Constable Scott Biser. He helped me iron out police procedures and if there is anything wrong in this book, that's my fault, and not his.

Thank you to Constable Jay Hall. He helped me with the K9 aspects of this novel. The training, the tracking, and the lack of resources. Once again, whatever is wrong in this book is my fault, not his.

Thank you to Constable Tom LeComte, who used to work in the nickel mines. You'll understand why when you get there in the book.

Special Mentions: So, Brandon McKenzie and Cameron McKeen, two fellas I work with, tried to get me to write a book called 'Unlucky Numbers'. I didn't write it, but it made its way into this tale.

OLIVIA

EDUCATION 1

"Where's mom?"

The killer's father turned his head to stare down at his son as he washed his hands at the sink. Sweat made circles in his armpits. The man scrubbed at the dirt and blood on his hands. To get at the blood under his fingernails, he used the brush normally used to clean the cast iron pan. The boy noticed the dirt. He noticed the blood. Not for the first time did the father think his son saw too much. He felt exposed, like being caught with his pecker out in public or something, with the same subtle layer of humiliation buoying up the uncomfortable feeling. It made him feel vulnerable. He didn't like feeling that way. Not one bit.

He said, "She's gone. She left. And she's never coming back."

He turned off the water and snatched a towel off the oven handle. He dried his hands, pretended to squint at what might remain under his nails while he took stock of his son staring at him with calm scrutiny. No eight-year-old should look like that. What was going on behind those eyes?

The boy looked outside the kitchen door that led to the backyard. A shovel leaned against a tree. Earlier this morning, the boy had seen the shovel in the tool shed when he had put away the lawnmower.

He took in his father drying his hands on the towel that moments ago had been white. Dirt marked the towel in finger-long swipes.

The boy, who knew what death was, who knew a lot more than an eight-year-old boy should know, nodded and said, "She said she was going to take me to the library. To get a library card. You'll have to do that now."

"We'll go tomorrow. How does that sound?"

The boy nodded, and before he turned away from his father, his eyes flitted to the shovel.

-1-

Summer of 2016

Morning light bled slowly upward onto the dark sky, a thumbnail of light blue pushing away the night and the stars to let them rest for the day. Sitting on the tailgate of his pick-up truck, smoking a Captain Black mini cigar, he stared into the infinite sky, feeling insignificant and supremely lucky at the same time. He read somewhere; he couldn't remember the source right now, maybe a Harvard professor? This professor estimated there were ten million, million, million balls of light, like the one creeping up from the other side of this world right now. About one in a million of those millions of suns have planets around them. Of all those, maybe one in a million, million has the right elements, temperature, what have you, to support life. Now, he didn't know what to think of all that sometimes. The scale of the universe, and what life teemed in it. How many of those lights up in the sky right now have planets surrounding them? Was there some alien out there, sitting on their version of a pick-up truck, smoking their version of a cigar, staring at their morning sky, wondering the why of it all? The why of anything? Were they looking at each other right now through an ocean of space? No. It doesn't work that way. Turns out the speed of light isn't all that speedy, not in the vastness of the universe and if he was say, looking in the direction of another alien, he'd be looking far into the past because, by the time the light carrying the image reached him, a countless number of years would have passed. He smiled, exhaled a plume, and told himself he should've been a philosopher. To be alive, well, that's the luckiest goddamn thing to occur to any person or animal for that matter. Look at the odds of life itself existing in the universe. Winning the lottery seems almost a sure thing compared to those long odds. That's the miracle, right there. Being alive. That's the special part. Now take good ole' planet Earth. Over four and a half billion years old. It took another billion years, give or take, for the first single cell organism to appear from the primordial soup. Fast forward a few more billion years until roughly two hundred thousand years ago and the first modern human comes along, add in a monstrous volcanic eruption that almost wiped-out humankind, and a comet that almost did the same years later, and now, well, here we are. It staggered him sometimes to think of all the obstacles that had to be overcome in order for him to be here, to be alive, and to even be sentient. And for that reason alone, what limited time was allotted to him he'd take full advantage of. He really appreciated life, the gift of it, the rarity of it, the miracle of it. And that's why it gave him so much pleasure to take someone else's life away. A precious, almost impossible gift being snatched away. The spark forever extinguished by his hands, by his design. Just thinking about it gave him an erection.

The red tip of the cigar flared. He exhaled, dropped the butt, crushed the ember under his heel, and glanced at his watch. Time to set up. He picked up the plastic cigar butt and put it in a plastic baggie to throw out later. He didn't leave anything DNA-related at a scene. He rubbed his hands together, slid off the tailgate, and shifted his shoulders, stretching them out. He slid on a hiker's pack, snapped the belt around his waist, and lifted a duffel bag from the truck bed. It'd take him, what, twenty minutes to get to his spot? He had timed it when he scouted it. He learned the hard way not to hike too far from his truck. He closed his eyes, inhaled the morning air, and smiled. He'd waited so long. Maybe today would be the day.

-2-

Bibi Khan stopped at the top of the trail, sweat running down her face and stinging her eyes. She put her hands on her hips and her open mouth sucked in oxygen. Although she wanted to sit down on the trail and relax for a bit, she knew if she did, she wouldn't be getting up anytime soon. And to sit on her ass, sweating through her Lululemon shorts, and lightweight top with her camera in her backpack not being used to capture this amazing, gorgeous Canadian scenery wasn't on the agenda. The agenda, the goal, was to capture images, upload them to her growing blog (Bibi's Forgotten Trails) to make people's jaws drop, their eyes round with envy and get people talking about her site. And maybe, just maybe, with a little luck and with Allah's blessing, monetize her site and make her living from hiking and photographing nature untouched by human hands. To live outdoors, to explore this beautiful country, and get paid for it? That's the dream. That's her hope. So instead of sitting down and giving in to what she would call her temptation to lazy town, she stood straight, inhaled for a count of four and exhaled until her heart settled into a comfortable rhythm. She slid her backpack around to her front and opened it. She grimaced as the sweat the backpack had trapped ran down her spine into her shorts.

"Gross."

She drank from her sparkling pink metal water bottle, capped it, and rolled the cool metal along her forehead. Through a gap in the trees, she could see how high she had climbed. A sky-blue truck with frowns of rust over the back tire and a MEC sticker on the back window was parked far below and was no bigger than her fingernail from this height. It was the one she passed in the public parking lot on her way up the trail. She could squeeze it between her fingers. She lifted her hand, put her thumb under the truck and her index finger above. She pinched them together and said, "Squish."

She loved it out here and if she could buy a cabin in the woods to live in (one without lurking killers or forbidden books to read), she'd be eternally happy. No city smells out here. Nothing but the scent of trees (she could actually smell the pine trees), the tweeting of birds, and the swish of branches and leaves as tiny animals searched for food.

Bibi put her water bottle away and removed a booklet and opened it to a page she had tabbed with a blue sticky note. This was the map page. She unfolded the map and traced her finger along the route she had taken so far and stopped where she thought she was.

"I'm close."

On the map, she noticed the trail flattened out for a hundred yards or so before it descended. The trail branched off at different points and lead to different locations. The main one, the trail most travelled and therefore, the one most cleared and easy to walk, would take her back around to the little parking area down there, the one with the pick-up truck. Boring! She wanted the trails least travelled! Where only the curious dared to venture! She wasn't worried about getting lost. She had that covered. Her phone had great reception and the GPS on it was ridiculously accurate and say, for whatever reason, she lost service and couldn't use her phone to help her navigate, she had a map, a compass, paper and pencil and she knew how to use them. Sweat plopped onto the map. Rummaging in her bag, she pulled out a hand towel, used it to dry off her face and forehead, and stuffed it back inside.

"Where was I?"

Using her finger, she traced ahead on the squiggly line representing the trail and saw four more offshoots that either ended because the trail ended or because the map people couldn't be bothered following every little trail. Hmm. She opened her book to the green tab and studied the Google map satellite image. Couldn't see much more of these trails through the trees. Who knew where the trails led to? By the end of the day, Bibi would know. And later on, so would her blog followers. And then, sponsorship by Patagonia, Merrell, and the best beverage container makers in the world (in her humble opinion), Yeti!

She put the maps back in their corresponding tabbed pages, confident she could find each trail as she walked ahead. She drank more water while eating a Cliff bar and when she was done, she put her wrapper in a garbage bag and her bottle in a side pocket. She mopped her face one last time and put the towel away. Now, time to take some awe-inspiring pictures.

•   •   •

She found the first trail under a low overhanging branch. She moved it out of
the way with splayed fingers. She ducked underneath and proceeded into the
shade. An animal trail petered off maybe fifty feet away toward a wall of densely
packed trees. Nothing here. She backed out, disappointed, shrugged it off, and
continued on. The next trail would accommodate her nicely. This trail was made
by humans and ran snake-like through small tree sprouts, rocks, and under the
roots of larger trees encroaching incrementally onto the path. Sunlight spilled
through the breaks in the canopy of leaves overhead like pillars of wavering gold.
Bibi smiled. This trail might lead somewhere special.

-3-
EDUCATION 2

Blood covered his arms to the elbows. His father stood off to the side, a rifle cradled in his elbow, the barrel pointed to the sky.

The killer scooped out the intestines of the deer he had shot. They didn't have a license, were hunting out of season (his father didn't believe in rules), and they typically field-dressed the animals and took whatever meat they could carry in their backpacks. The killer was the one who had taken down the deer. Whoever made the kill, dressed the kill. It was a rule between them. One stood guard in case a conservation officer heard the shot and decided to investigate. He hurried with the cleaning. He wasn't sloppy about it. Fast and efficient, but not sloppy. His father would never allow lazy work. After the guts were removed, the killer skinned the animal. Next, he went to sectioning the joints.

His father lit a cigarette, exhaled and said, "I don't understand this notion of freedom."

The killer paused in his work and wiped away the sweat from his forehead. He left a red smear. He didn't mind his father's little speeches. He'd heard this one before and expected colourful vitriol to add further entertainment, and although he knew his father was crazy, crazy in the should-be-locked-up-forever-or-he'll-kill-someone (like his mother) sort of way, he didn't entirely disagree with him on some of his opinions. Even crazy people can be right from time to time.

"The only freedom a man has in this country is if he pays for it, right? You don't pay your taxes and guess what? They take your home. If you still don't pay your taxes, they could even take your right to mobility, like it says in the Charter, by tossing you in jail." He shook his head and inhaled as though he wanted to punish the cigarette, "They want everything in exchange for this 'freedom' they talk about. How is that free? Say you want to drive the roads, right? You need a driver's license to do that, and you need to tell them everything about you to get it. You have to tell them who you are, how old you are, where you live, and heaven help you

if you can't prove it with some other form of government document! And once you give them everything, once they have their finger up your ass and crooking it to pull you in, you have to pay for the 'privilege' of driving. What a crock of shit! Look at us here, right now, out hunting to provide for ourselves. Doing this, the most natural thing mankind has done since the time they crawled out of the ocean and stood up and started hunting for their family, and, well guess, what? You need a license to hunt, too. And you also have to only hunt when they say you can! They've chained our freedom to the table legs of bureaucracy, is what they did. The best thing a person can do is to not be the person they think you are you know? Be a bunch of people. That way, to nail you, they have to nail them all. Keep them confused. That's the best tactic. Freedom lies in not existing at all. They can't incarcerate smoke. Be vapour."

The killer frowned. A new twist on an old speech. He pointed his knife at his father and said, "You know, that might be the smartest thing you've ever said."

He snorted. Smoke streamed from his nostrils. He said, "What the fuck does a teenage turd like you know?"

The father tried to downplay the compliment only it didn't work. The killer's father was right. He did see everything. He knew the compliment (was it one?) touched the pride button in his father's chest. He tagged the knowledge in his head. He could do that, highlight an idea, tell himself to remember it, and he would remember it for a long time. The ability would have helped him in school if his father had ever sent him. He tagged the idea because it was useful to remember a tool that would help him manipulate his father.

• • •

He positioned himself in a way so that he could see far along the path in both directions. He wanted someone alone and wanted to see if anyone might be following close behind. Sometimes in these summer months, the trails teemed with hikers. Teens looking for a spot to smoke drugs, couples looking for a spot to make out, and families walking along, trying to find that ever-elusive family time to spend together. The families amused him the most. He'd see one of the parents smiling, ploughing ahead, pointing around and exclaiming about the sights, and a teenager would be walking with phone in hand, earbuds in, and nodding along to whatever music happened to be playing, with a younger sibling on their heels holding a stick and swiping at the passing branches. Because of how busy the trails could be, the summer months tended to be the most frustrating time to catch prey. But that made it random. And random was good. Random was almost undetectable. There had been times when he had spent days in a spot and walked away empty-handed. Disappointing? Sure. It also added to the excitement. He didn't know whom he would find if anyone. The anticipation was tantalizing.

Today, he'd been motionless in this spot for almost four hours. Once he settled in and became a part of the scenery, the animals soon went back to their business. He'd seen deer, rabbits, and once, in a different place at a different time, he'd seen a bear. That was something else. A giant furry predator, lumbering through, cracking branches as thick as his thigh as it passed by, and he hoped those amber eyes would take no interest in him. The bear had seen him, knew he was there. He was sure of that. Thankfully, it took no more interest in him than it would an ant. It yawned, ivory teeth bigger than piano keys, shook itself and moved on. He dreamed about that bear every once in a while. In his dreams, the bear did take an interest in him. Sometimes it chased him, sometimes it caught him, and always before those jaws closed over the top of his skull he'd wake up, sweating, cursing, but also grateful it had only been a dream. Grateful to be alive.

He thought maybe today might be one of those unfortunate days. When the randomness of events wouldn't work in his favour. Even though it was still early in the day, in his time waiting here, he hadn't seen anyone. Unusual, it being summer and all. He thought he'd at least see trail runners or a hiker or two. So far, nothing. This was a patience game. A game of discipline. And he liked to test himself. He thought returning home empty-handed wouldn't be so bad, until a moving dot appeared through the branches dripping with leaves in front of him, putting to lie his nonchalant attitude toward an unsuccessful hunt.

He couldn't tell if the person was a male, female or other because of the thickness of the brush and his position. And really, he couldn't have cared less. He was an equal opportunity killer and had always thought racism to be inherently stupid. DNA had proven we all came from the same people, the same place. In this day and age, being negative toward any race was really just being negative toward yourself, or toward your own ancestors. We're all the same under the skin. And he knew that to be true from personal experience. He'd peeled off a person's skin before. Flaying, they called it back in the day. All he wanted from the person approaching him on the trail was for them to be alone. His stomach tingled.

He gritted his teeth. A bug landed on his cheek and crawled toward his eye. He remained still. A statue of concentration. The bug flew off. The person approached. It was a woman with a hiker's backpack. The backpack had the same colour scheme as a MEC one he'd been eyeballing for some time, waiting for it to go on sale. A sturdy canvas construct useful for this hobby of his. The woman stopped about ten feet from him. She peered down through a break in the trees and he thought, *she sees me! She's staring right at me!* And then she turned her attention to her backpack and his heart returned to a normal rhythm. He moved his tongue around to have the moisture return to his arid mouth. Behind her, the path remained empty of people. And to the front of her, no one. Would she be his next project? He had an interesting plan for her demise. While she opened a map, drank water, and wiped the sweat from her head, he inched forward, ever so slowly, closing the distance.

-4-

Bibi parted branches with her hands, stepped over divots, balanced on rocks, moving through the woods as graceful as a wood sprite from a magical world. She heard water ahead. Not the quiet burbling of a small river. This sounded more substantial. Not quite a waterfall torrent, but… something. She followed the sound, having left the trail to do so. She could only hear the water now. The sound obscured her own movements through the woods, her stepping on leaves and brittle sticks. She walked for some time following the sound of water. She glanced back over her shoulder and couldn't even see where the main trail might be. The water sound drew her on, further and further away from the primary path. She parted a screen of leaves, her eyes protruded, and she said, "Yes!"

She found the source of the water. A run-off of water spilling into a hole, or the top of a cave system (she didn't know) and hitting an unseen bottom with a bass rumble. The hole was four, five feet across, and resembled a not-quite triangle, with jagged rock sides and soft greenery running around the edges. It was beautiful and since she hadn't read about it from any guidebook of this area or hadn't heard of it from other adventure bloggers, she knew it was her find. Bibi followed the water back with her eyes and couldn't see where it was coming from. Maybe another cave system? Or just a deep recess in the rock wall that bordered part of this area? She'd like to know. She'd like to find out. And she'd love to share her experience with her audience and get one step closer to lucrative sponsorships!

She slipped her backpack to the ground safely away from the dark hole and opened the top. Did she have a light in here for her camera bright enough to penetrate the darkness? To see what was down there, if anything? Her fingers tingled, and she couldn't help but smile. This was turning out to be an excellent day.

Off to her side in her peripheral vision, something rose from the ground, something green, something bristling with branches like the back of a porcupine. Her stomach dropped as she turned to face the threat, this thing emerging from the very earth. It hit her before she could raise a hand. The first hit exploded stars behind her eyes. Drool shot from her mouth, and she shook her head to clear it. Too late. She was hit again. She blinked and she was looking at a blue square of sky through the overhead foliage. She blinked again and then the green, bristly monster stood above her. She tried to move but the world spun, her stomach flipped, and darkness bled across her vision.

●   ●   ●

She was conscious of the water running before anything else. She felt the coolness of the nearby air against her cheek, and she groaned. It was then she noticed something was in her mouth, something pressing against her tongue with a rough fabric feel to it. She blinked her eyes open and the pain forced her to squeeze them closed again. The light was too bright, incandescent daggers piercing her eyes to scrape at her brain. Bibi exhaled through her nose. She remembered. The thing rising from the ground. Her whole body felt dipped in ice water. A shiver vibrated her entire body. And in that shiver, she noticed she couldn't move her hands or her feet. Wait. That's not true. She could move them, articulate her wrists and ankles a bit, but that was all. She couldn't move them apart. Her heart deep thudded. Bibi opened her eyes. The monster leaned over her.

It spoke, "You're awake. Earlier than I thought. You're a tough one. That's good."

She couldn't see a face. It was draped in the shadow produced by what he was wearing. It wasn't a monster. It was a man. But then, plenty of men have turned out to be monsters, haven't they? Either way, she wasn't safe. This man wasn't here to help.

"I bet you're wondering what's happening, huh? I'm going to wait until it's dark, and when it is, I'm going to carry you to my truck. I'm going to bring you somewhere, and I'm going to kill you. All I want from you is to keep still and to keep quiet. That's it. If you don't, I'll hurt you. I'll hurt you real bad." He produced a knife, seemingly from thin air, but she knew it could easily have been hidden in the shadows draping him. He let the sunlight catch the blade and reflected the light into her eyes. Bibi caught a scent of smoke, not like a cigarette, but something different, more aromatic. She turned her head and closed her eyes. He said, "And if you don't, if you're still stubborn enough to test me after I've hurt you, I'm going to cut out your tongue, and I'm going to toss it down that hole you were so fond of. The same place I tossed your phone."

Tears collected in her eyes. A couple of her friends knew where she had been planning to go today. That wouldn't help her now though. Bibi was an experienced hiker. They wouldn't start worrying about her until tomorrow at the earliest. By then, it would be too late.

• • •

The sun was gone. Shining on another face on the other side of the world. Maybe highlighting the edges of incoming waves on a beach with someone watching the rising sun and enjoying the moment or maybe they were staring at their phone, ignoring their one shot at life in order to see the next meme, the next TikTok or Instagram post. Watching other people living. He sighed. That was their problem, choosing to waste this miracle of life. He was living his life to the fullest. And when he finally did die, he could say he spent his time well. He peered down at the woman, Bibi, after having read her name from her driver's license, while he waited for the night.

"Well, I guess it's about that time."

He took off his ghillie suit with branches and leaves interwoven through the netting and put them in the duffel bag. From his backpack, he removed his night-vision goggles and secured them to his head. He turned them on, and the night turned to day. Well, a green-tinted day, but nevertheless, he could see. And now comes the hard part. Carrying someone out was not only physically hard over dangerous terrain, but it was also the only time he could potentially be caught. There was no reasonable explanation for carrying a bound person out of the woods. If someone saw him, they'd question him, or if they didn't, they'd at least call the cops. No one else should be on these trails this late at night in this darkness. Even with a flashlight, it would be hard to see and navigate the terrain. It was dangerous and not worth risking an injury if the person happened to walk off the trail to fall down a steep, unforgiving decline. Experienced backpackers rarely travelled at night for that very reason. In his case, he could only move his prey at night. It was the best way to minimize risk. It was one of his 'rules for not getting caught for multiple murders'. Random people, random places, and no places with potential surveillance cameras, no places or times with potential witnesses and leave no evidence behind. And that included the body. As far as he knew, the police didn't know a killer like him even existed. By the lack of concerted effort or news stories, he believed the police thought all the missing people, from different trails and forests, were unrelated.

He carried the backpack and duffel bag closer to the main trail. He marked a tree with his knife (it glowed a bright white with his goggles) and put the bags behind it. He returned for Bibi, as he planned to sling her over his shoulder and carry her to his truck, and saw her shimmying on her stomach to the hole where he'd thrown her phone.

"Shit!"

He ran to her, saw the soles of her shoes, and noticed with mounting horror that the top half of her body was already in the hole. He dove, reaching for her, thinking, *I'm not going to make it, not going to make it!* He hit the ground with a breath-stealing 'oomph' and his right hand clamped onto her boot.

"Gotcha!"

And then the boot slid off her foot and Bibi shimmied down the hole.

"Shit, shit, shit! C'mon man!"

He scrambled to the hole and peered inside. Night vision goggles work by amplifying ambient light available. In this hole in the earth, there wasn't a lot of light to amplify. He couldn't see her. He couldn't see if the hole led anywhere. If it led into a cavern, or another pool, or whatever, he didn't know. Bibi was gone.

"Fuck!"

He couldn't leave her behind. Especially prey that was gagged with bound hands and feet. If she was found, that would definitely draw attention. But what could he do? Return in the morning? Hope to see more then and reassess? Was that his only real option here? Bibi pulled a fast one on him. He kind of admired her in a way. Pissed at her too, but in there, mixed with it, if he was being honest with himself, he liked her grit. Her only options had been to go with him or dive into that hole, and she *chose the hole.* Man. He knew she was a tough one, but not that tough. He had underestimated her. He stood, staring into the hole. He should add a new rule. 'Never leave the day's catch alone, even for a minute'. He shook his head and tossed her boot in after her. He strained to hear it splash. He didn't hear anything. Maybe the sound of the running water was louder than other sounds, or maybe the hole was too deep. That could be a good thing. Hopefully, no one would ever find her.

He checked the ground, looking for anything he might have left behind. And seeing nothing, with a sigh, he returned to the tree, picked up his gear, and walked to his truck. Once or twice, he looked back, recriminations for his lack of foresight zinging through his mind. It was done. No point worrying about it anymore. He told himself to make sure he learned from this. The thought didn't make it hurt any less.

-5-

"Well, I guess it's about that time."

Bibi twitched. Her heart sprinted within her breast. If he took her out of here, she was a dead woman. She knew it. He had told her as much. It wasn't like he was trying to keep her in suspense or tell her if she cooperated, she might make it out alive. He told her he was going to kill her.

The man stood. She heard the distinct sound of a zipper opening followed by other rustling sounds. Within a minute or so, the man started walking away. Bibi froze.

Was he leaving her here? He said he'd be carrying her out of here. She squinted her eyes, thinking for some reason that would make her hear better. Unfortunately, the sound of the water prevented her from hearing him moving through the woods after a few feet. How long did she have before he returned? She remembered the hole being quite a distance from the main path. But was he going there or to his truck? Did it matter? What could she do about it anyway? Nothing. There was not a thing she could do.

She turned her head toward the hole. She couldn't see it. But she could hear the water and she knew where the hole was. She *could* do something, couldn't she? She could crawl into that hole before he came back and… what? Drown? Crack her skull open on some rocks? Or get pinned in some crevasse and suffocate? Yeah, but what was he going to do to her? Bibi read horror books. She watched horror movies. She could be in for a world of pain. Or what about those poor women who had escaped that rape house? The women who had been held captive for years and tortured and raped. That could happen to her. That could be who this man was. One of those nutjobs. No, no. Both of those guys are dead now. That woman killed them both. Bibi had just read about that recently. That woman had survived. But so many other women in that house didn't survive. And that was no horror movie. That was real life.

Bibi turned onto her stomach, tucked her elbows underneath her and told herself to go. Don't think about it, just go. She scooted forward. Not fast, but at least forward, getting closer to the hole. She felt the coolness of the water on her face. Her hands scraped over the rocks along the rim.

"Shit!"

The gag pressed against her tongue as a cry tried to escape her. She used the rim to pull herself further into the hole, and then swung herself from side to side, using momentum to bring her further forward. She shimmied and pulled and felt her hips at the rim, then the tops of her thighs.

"Gotcha!"

Pressure on her foot inside her boot. Bibi groaned and squirmed forward. Her foot pulled free from her boot and she fell into the hole.

A scream reverberated in her throat, muffled by the gag as she shot her bound hands out in front of her. She didn't travel far when the binding between her wrists caught on a rock overhang. It arrested her fall for a second, but the lower half of her body kept going and swung her around so that she was now facing up toward the hole. The sharp walls gouged her skin through her clothes, peeled back layers of flesh along her cheek, and ripped at the exposed skin of her arms, legs and shins. She kept sliding until her body settled sideways, in a fissure with her feet slightly higher than her head. The cold water splashed onto her navel and ran under her, soaking her buttocks. She peered up to the hole and couldn't see it. She must be under an overhang. That's good, right? Not being able to see the way out means someone looking in the hole shouldn't be able to see her. She closed a right eye as blood flowing from her forehead slid into it. It didn't matter. It was so dark in here she couldn't see a thing. What did she need her eyes for?

She felt, rather than saw, something pass by her from above. She had no idea it was her own boot. Not that she would have cared.

•　　•　　•

During the long night in the hole, after she had used her bound hands to twist and remove the gag that had been crammed in her mouth and then secured by tape wrapped around her head, she dozed in fits and spurts, shivering from the cold water hitting her body. She hissed as the tape pulled strands of hair from her scalp and added the pain to a long list of complaints her body was making because of the injuries sustained in her fall. She was terrified of falling asleep and had fought it with every fibre of strength she possessed, which, after all she had gone through so far, let's say her reserves were almost depleted. One moment, not sure if her eyes were open or not because of the darkness, she thought she heard someone breathing behind her ear. She should have known that was impossible. The man couldn't be behind her and with the ambient water noise, there would be no plausible way that she would be able to hear him. That didn't stop her mouth from going dry or prevent the sharp insertion of adrenaline into her veins, electrifying her limbs and raising the BPM of her heart. All night long the impossible became possible in her overtired brain. Her imagination in overdrive, stoked and fueled with the continuing remembrance of the shape rising from the forest floor. That shouldn't have been possible. The woods coming alive and reaching for her, knocking her out, and tying her up. But it happened. Would she ever stop seeing that? Would the man chase her every night in her dreams only to disappear with her death, hopefully many, many years into the future? She hoped not. She stifled a sob. Choked on a hiccough threatening to shift into a crying session. She didn't want to cry. Not now. She worried if she started to cry, she wouldn't be able to stop. Crying for an eternity in this abyss. It seemed possible, probable even. She told herself to stop brooding, wait for more light, and think of a way out of this mess. She had made it this far, right?

•　　•　　•

It took a minute or two for Bibi to realize she could see. What had once been complete darkness (or as her friend Rori of Irish descent would say, dark as a coal miner's butthole), she now saw shadows growing from the walls. The rock wall became a blue, jagged milieu, blurry but with every passing moment becoming more distinct.

I'm fucked.

The light didn't help at all. In fact, it only made it clear to Bibi she was in deep trouble. The deepest trouble she could be in after escaping the forest man. She couldn't see the hole, but she knew where it was because of the sunlight hitting the walls and reflecting it into her squinting eyes. When she fell, she must have ricocheted off one wall to land in this crack although she didn't remember feeling it at the time. She remembered her wrists getting stuck and her body swinging and then being stopped by hitting something solid. Her hands and feet were still bound by the large plastic zip ties. She tried to rub the plastic against the rocks but couldn't move her hands around or get a sharp piece of the rock wall in between her wrists to even saw, hack or rip at the plastic. She couldn't get free and she sure wasn't going to try to go deeper, go *further* underground to see if there was a way out of here. No way.

She could try screaming. Calling for help. She shivered. What if he was still up there? Waiting there for her to poke her head out like a hedgehog from a hole. As patient as he had been during the day while he waited for the night to fall. Not speaking to her, not even looking at her half the time. The man was the embodiment of patience. And even if he wasn't there, so what? She had gone far off the main path. Who else, other than her, would be stupid enough to go adventuring off path? No one would hear her. She had doomed herself.

She started crying. She was going to die down here. She escaped one death only to run right into another. Stupid adventure blog. She was right about one thing. She really couldn't stop crying once she got going.

•　　•　　•

BUZZ.

Bibi jerked awake and moaned. Everywhere hurt. There wasn't an uninjured spot on her body. Blood trickled anew down her face. She must have opened a cut on her head when she had woken up.

BUZZ.

"Ahh!"

The top of her left shoulder blade vibrated.

"What?"

BUZZ.

Her phone? How could that be? The man said he… tossed it in the hole. Had she been sleeping on it all night?

BUZZ.

Who cares about the how? Bibi, turned, grunted, shimmied, squealed, muttered, "Fuck," trying her best to get at the phone underneath her own shoulder blade. She felt tears welling. She couldn't get at it. Stuck in the crevasse, she couldn't turn, couldn't bend, couldn't get the only thing that could save her.

"This can't be real."

Bibi pressed her shoulder blade against the phone.

BUZZ.

"I know! I'm trying!"

Using her shoulder, she drew the phone down toward her waist. She lifted her shoulder above the phone, pinned it, and drew it down, over and over until she felt it just above her waist, under her ribs. She reached for it with her tied hands. Her fingers scratched at dirt, but she was close. Her fingers crabbed for it. So close. She moaned. The nearness of the phone, tormenting her. Tears welled; snot ran freely… there.

She pinched the phone with thumb and forefinger and gingerly lifted it, hoping it didn't slide out from between her grasp. She glanced at the screen.

Text from Rori: *Where r u girl? The lil prick O bombed a tittie pic I sent, wtf?*

Bibi laughed, cried, sobbed, and called her friend Rori.

-6-

EDUCATION PART 3

"Heard you coming from a mile away."

His father pointed a rifle at a conservation officer. The barrel wasn't more than four feet away from the young, sweating officer sporting a thin, juvenile moustache. That was what the killer remembered most about the man, his moustache. How could he not know how foolish it looked? Why would anyone walk around like that? Then he looked at his father. The long greasy hair, the matted and uneven beard, and the teeth as yellow as corn kernels. But his father was different. He'd been swinging from the crazy tree for some time now.

His father said, "Get on your knees. Hands above your head, too asshole. And don't even think of going for your gun."

The officer knelt. He raised his arms straight up, as though he were reaching for the clouds.

"Anyone else with you? Any friends going to happen along soon?"

The sweaty moustache man shook his head no.

"Isn't that a sad day for you?"

His father, a wiry, skinny man, lowered the rifle and pushed it to his back to hang down on the strap as he removed a hunting knife from a sheath tied to the outside of his right thigh. Before the conservation man could lower his arms or utter a sound of protest, his father buried the knife to the hilt in the man's chest. Conservation officers wore bulletproof vests. Knives have no trouble getting through them the way pistol and shotgun rounds do. The knife went through the vest as though there was no vest at all.

The officer's mouth opened and closed. He blinked and looked down at the knife, blink-blink-blink, and with his arms still straight up, he fell over on his side. After a few seconds, he stopped air-gasping like a fish.

The killer tingled all over his body. He almost dropped his rifle. His pores felt wide, huge even, and the hairs rolled upright on his body like fans at a baseball game doing the wave. His erection pressed against the zipper of his jeans.

"What are you gawping at? Get over here and give me a hand? We gotta make this fucker disappear."

They knew the land well. They carried the officer two kilometres to an old, dry riverbed. The water had eroded the earth under a large oak tree and that's where they stuffed the officer. They gathered heavy rocks and covered him to prevent animals from getting at him and bringing pieces of him out to maybe get found. Unlikely to occur but why risk it when all it would take was a little initial work? After they buried the officer, they made their way home staying off the main trails to avoid the possibility of being seen. His father smoked cigarette after cigarette only pausing through inhalations to cough.

"Why did you kill him?"

His father shrugged, "He saw us. We don't have a license. Easier to kill him than deal with a fine."

He knew the answer, he knew it when he was eight, but he asked anyway, not totally understanding why, he said, "Did you kill mom?"

His father stopped. The cigarette dangling from his lip curled smoke into his eyes, causing him to squint.

He said, "I told you she left."

"I remember. And she's never coming back."

"No. She isn't."

•　　•　　•

When he saw Bibi on the TV being escorted into a police station with a foil blanket wrapped around her, to say he was surprised would have been the understatement of the century. If a leprechaun popped out of his sink and offered him a pot of gold, he wouldn't have been more surprised. Was that an exaggeration? No. In this instance, that would be a big, fat, no. Part of it had to do with the fact that his murder run had been flawless so far. The critical part of himself, the portion of his soul, brain, whatever, that was always reminding himself to be careful, don't get cocky, stay humble man, stay humble, knew this was a possibility. He couldn't expect to continue doing what he was doing without some cracks appearing in the well-constructed wall he had built using his carefully selected rules as the mortar. But he did expect it. He told himself not to, but he did anyway. He expected to go on for as long as he drew breath in his body. And that epiphany surprised him just as much as seeing Bibi on the TV.

"This is good. It's good to know your weaknesses."

It didn't feel good, though. It hurt. The realization didn't just bruise his ego, it had taken a baseball bat to it with vigour. And his battered ego wasn't even the real problem. He had killed eleven people over the years, and no one knew a murderer existed. The people he had murdered were presumed missing. Lost in the wilderness, dead of exposure or misadventure and picked apart and eaten by the many scavengers making the woods their home. But now the police knew a man had hidden in the woods and waited for the right opportunity to abduct and to kill. Would they tie this incident to any of the others in the past?

There had been that one person who saw him a long time ago. When he was still learning and refining his technique. What park had that been in? Shanocktuk? Something like that. He shook his head with a smile tugging at his lips. He internally cringed at the memory even though he smiled. He was so new, so… unprofessional, it was embarrassing to remember it. That was odd in itself. Being embarrassed about practicing how to abduct and murder someone.

He had been hiding in a bush wearing gear similar to what he had now, but not as sophisticated. An amateur's attempt at being a professional and thinking (that was the funny part, the hardy-har part that at the time wasn't funny at all), he was well hidden and could stay there all day with people passing by and none of them being any wiser.

"What are you doing?"

He gasped, turned and saw two teenagers, a boy and a girl. The girl held a Slurpee cup in her hand, the red straw just under her bottom lip. The boy, almost a man really, probably a football player with those wide shoulders, wearing a backpack with straps looking like strings on him. The boy looked at him and frowned. The girl wore a bemused expression, as though she had something to say, something smartass but worried about saying anything to an adult stranger. It was the boy who had asked the question. The squeaking at the end of the question indicating he was still in development, still a maturing work in progress.

"Nothing. I was waiting for a friend."

The girl: "You gonna scare them?"

"Yeah. That was the plan."

He said it, knew it sounded shaky as though he were clinging to their suggestion rather than scaring a friend being the actual reason he was hiding out in the bush. The girl laughed maybe imagining how fun it would be to hide out and pop up in front of a friend, but the boy? He didn't buy it. At least the boy's expression gave the impression he didn't believe the killer's excuse. Not at all. They continued on their walk, the girl's voice a lilting soundtrack fading with every step they took. The boy looked back at him once before disappearing behind a turn on the trail.

He was embarrassed. He didn't know them and yet the embarrassment filled his face with blood. He had been spotted *and* he hadn't heard them sneak up on him. He had no idea they were there. He knew he needed more work on his camouflage, and he definitely needed to develop his positioning. He needed to see as much of the trail as possible before settling in. He had made mistakes, but he learned from them. Being embarrassed sucked and he never wanted to feel that way again as long as he was open enough to learn from his errors, these instances of idiocy would happen less and less. He had left the park after removing his camouflage and he knew that if he had a tail, he would have tucked between his legs. He had been seen, so the day was over. If someone was to go missing from this park, and it made the news and that boy remembered seeing a bushman, then that would be problematic.

That misstep had been nothing compared to this one. Now here was Bibi telling the world about him. The police would now know someone like him existed. Would they think about other missing people on other forested trails? There was no reason to tie Bibi's attempted abduction to other missing people, but that didn't mean they wouldn't. Something to think about.

It never occurred to him to go after Bibi. He never tied himself to his prey with emotion. She had gotten the better of him, but he didn't take it personally. He was the one who fucked it up. It wasn't the 'who' he killed that mattered, only the killing did. The taking of their life and the fact that they knew he was going to take their life, that was the high, the drug, the addiction spiking his blood. Nothing else came close to it. Not skydiving (he'd tried that once), and no, not even sex. No comparison. It was like the two concepts, sex and murder, didn't even exist on the same planet. They were so far apart from each other on the satisfaction meter. Besides, going after Bibi would be stupid. Watching her on the TV, surrounded by cameras, microphones pushed toward her face. She looked fearful, like a nervous kitten or something. He wasn't fooled by her though. She was no kitten, not by a long shot. She was a tiger. And you don't fuck with nervous tigers.

He turned off the TV, glanced at his watch. Time to work out. He put on his headphones, selected an 80s hip-hop list on Spotify, and turned on the treadmill.

-7-

Bibi's interview with the police was thorough. It took two days to get all the details down, including all descriptors, distinctive smells, words and phrases used by the woodsman and his methodology. She knew they had combed the area where she had been attacked, looking for any discarded evidence. They went all-in on their search for evidence. They didn't find evidence in relation to him, the woodsman (as Bibi thought of him), but they found her boot at the bottom of the hole. She wanted to ask how they retrieved her boot, thought she might sound stupid, and let the question go.

Bibi made a point of describing the pick-up truck in the lot, replete with the rust and the MEC sticker. The detectives recorded the information thoroughly. Because that pick-up truck was there didn't mean it was involved, but if that pick-up truck was described at another major case scene, a potential link could be drawn. All this information was entered into POWERCASE, a province-wide investigative database. If any other police service in Ontario had a similar case, it would alert the investigators to the similarity so they could contact the police service where the information originated from for further follow-up. The software had been mandated for use by Ontario police services after the Paul Bernardo case. This ensured all police services were connected and sharing their information so if someone were raping women in Toronto and that same someone was raping women in the city of Guelph; the similarities of the offences would be marked, and a link would be established, and the police would have double the investigative notes and leads to follow up on. No one wanted another Bernardo to happen again. The pick-up truck was entered, and no link emerged from within the ever-growing POWERCASE database. Bibi's case went cold.

-8-

WINTER OF 2020
EDUCATION PART 4

Their home sat on a half-acre lot. A two-storey home, an old farmhouse his father had bought years ago because of his distaste for city life and all it represented. From his father, he learned about investing. To look at him, you wouldn't think the man knew anything about anything. He had a wild look to him. The long hair, the beard, the stains on his shirts. He hadn't always been that way. He used to care about his appearance. He used to care about a lot of things, which, in looking back at the old photographs, he could see why his mother had been attracted to him in the first place. As his father's paranoia grew, the need for self-isolation expanded. He took them away from their suburban home to this home where the nearest neighbour couldn't be seen if you looked out a window. The killer didn't listen to his father about a lot of things. Such as the belief his father held that the government cared enough about him to spy on him. The paranoia persisted to such a degree at one point that his father cancelled their internet. He was convinced it was being used to track him, monitor him, and put ideas into his head. Since his father was an investor, the need to monitor his investments overpowered his paranoia and with great, pouting reluctance, he paid for the return of their access to the internet.

Once, after the murder of the conservation officer, his father sat him down in front of the computer and showed him their total worth. He pointed at the numbers with his index finger, a half-moon of dirt outlining the fingernail, and said, "This is the only real freedom. Money. I don't have to work for anyone. I don't have to eat a shit sandwich fed to me by some idiotic boss, and money, my boy, is the only real insulation against disaster. This determines the worth of a person within the structure of society and the rules they set up. Otherwise, they'll eat you alive. You been reading those books I gave you, right?"

"Yes." His father had handed him a stack of books on investing six months ago. They were interesting to read. Understanding that patience and time in investing, above all, could make a person rich seemed counterintuitive and different from what the movies tell you. Stocks are a gamble! Stay away! From what he read; it wasn't that way at all. Stay out of debt, invest for the long haul, and wealth, according to the statistics, would be inevitable.

In between reading the books his father insisted he study; he'd read everything else he could get his hands on from the online library. Tolstoy, Nietzsche, Hume, Shaw, Newton, Plato, Aristotle, and biographies of the great figures in history. He had a stack of notebooks filled with his own notations and musings on what he read as he tried to make sense of the ideas. The concepts watered and nourished his own notion of truth. The preciousness and rarity of human life while at the same time, the utter meaninglessness of it within the overall scope of nature and the scale of the universe. The universe didn't care about the lives of these sentient monkeys scurrying along on the surface of this rock hurtling through space that was one asteroid strike away from annihilation. The universe, nature, didn't care about anything at all. He thought more and more of this concept after the murder of the conservation officer. Trying to figure out how to find joy in a vacuum.

"Good. I'm going to give you some money, and I want you to make it grow. Think you can do that?"

"Yes."

"I think so too." He tapped the screen and said, "This here is the only education you'll ever need. And the more money you have, the more freedom you'll get."

Looking at the screen totalling their assets, the killer knew sooner or later, he'd kill his father for that money. He caught his father looking at him and he wondered, not for the first time, if his father could read his thoughts.

• • •

He was waiting for the snow to fall and when the first fat lazy drops fell from the darkening sky, shifting with the wind before settling on the ground, he sat by his window with a coffee in one hand and a book in the other. Once he saw that the snow was sticking and not melting into the ground, he waited some more. When the dark grass was coated white, he finished his coffee, put the book on the table beside him, stood and brought the empty cup to his kitchen. He rinsed it and put it in the dishwasher. He descended creaking wooden stairs to stop on the concrete basement floor, feeling the coldness on his toes and heels.

He flicked on the light and walked to the far corner of the room. The basement was a work in progress.

Studs outlined where future walls would be. Wires ran through the studs to electrical outlets. A stack of drywall lay flat on the floor in one corner. He wanted to create a workout room in the basement as well as have a place to work on some of his traps and methods of disposal. A workbench was pushed against a finished wall. Above the workbench was a pegboard with tools hung inside white outlines. On the bench sat a canvas duffel bag. Beside it was a backpack. His hunting gear was inside each bag. He slung the backpack over one shoulder and lifted the duffel bag with the other hand. He left the room, closing the doors behind him, whistling the tune from *The Andy Griffith Show* and thinking about the upcoming hunt.

• • •

He had caught a man. He placed himself adjacent to the trail, making sure he could see all approaches, like he had learned to do. He knew the spot. He had scouted it out before. He parked in the gravel lot of an old roadside diner, closed now because of COVID-19. If no one was leaving their homes, no one was partaking in the food of a roadside diner. Never mind that the place had been open thirty-four years and had never closed its doors. The only reason he knew of it was because they wrote about it online. People had tried to raise money for the place, to keep the doors open, and although everyone's heart was in the right place, it didn't work because a lot of people were out of work and had to worry about their own bills. It did provide the killer with a unique opportunity. The roadside diner, Louise's Eggstravaganza, catered to highway travellers and hikers using the popular trail that skirted the city of Waterloo. People still used the forest trails, even during the pandemic, but no one visited the diner. He could park there, around the back of the squat, red and white building and there'd be no one to see him. And more importantly, there were no cameras.

He arrived there in the middle of the night. In the darkness, he smoked his obligatory Captain Black cigar. When finished, he stubbed it out and placed the end in a small plastic bag to throw out later, far from here and nowhere near his home. It was dark enough and late enough for him to put on his camouflage hunting gear by his truck without worrying about being seen. When that was done, with one bag in hand, he walked to his spot, cognizant of the snow still falling heavily upon the ground. The weather would be useful in covering his tracks. He put the bag down on the ground and got into position and waited. The snow collected upon him. He felt it patter upon his white waterproof clothing, falling in soft waves. It was relaxing, hypnotic almost and he was comfortable. With his clothing, he didn't feel the cold at all. No, he liked the sight of the falling snow, the smell of the clean air, the absolute silence of the forest, and the transformation of the dark environment into a light one. He witnessed the tree branches getting heavy with accumulating snow, drooping under the added weight. Sometimes he'd hear the snow sliding off branches and hitting the ground with a muffled 'pumf' noise. He delighted in the moment. This one-of-a-kind, supremely unique, can't possibly be happening in this same way anywhere else in the universe experience. In this way, happy in the moment of his unlikely existence, he waited for his prey.

● ● ●

He heard the person before he saw them. The rhythmic crunching of someone running in the fresh snow, making new tracks, marring the crystalline surface. The sound pulled him out of his serene trance. He had anticipated the snowfall. The weather app on his phone told him as much, but it appeared that a lot more had fallen than was projected. He was under a deep blanket of snow. He had to constantly dig out the area around his eyes so that he could see. He had considered, after realizing how much snow had actually fallen, of leaving here thinking no one would venture out in this. To wait here would be a waste of time. He told himself he'd give it until nine am. If someone showed up before that time on a day like today, there would be a good chance they'd be alone. If he waited until after nine am, and people started venturing out, those odds wouldn't hold for long. Patience rewarded him.

The runner came along just before eight. It wasn't light out yet, the sky still had a dark blue cast to it, and shortly after hearing the person moving along, he saw a light bouncing along the ground. He was amazed the person could follow the snow-covered trail and thought anyone running through this deep snow on such a day was clearly obsessive and ran no matter what potential obstacles, weather included, were in the way. An obsessive would know the trail intimately. He hadn't been hopeful of catching anyone today. He thought it'd be a practice day to work out the kinks in a snow-ambush scenario. As the person approached, the killer raised his torso, put his hands underneath his shoulders, and situated his feet in a low-ready-sprinter-at-the-blocks type stance. The layer of snow hardly shifted from on top of him. The crunching feet drew closer and the runner (a man judging by the height and shoulders) came into view. The man wore a red toque with a headlamp strapped around his forehead. His bright orange jacket caught and reflected the errant light from the lamp. Plumes of breath escaped the man's open mouth as though he were a lumbering steam train moving along a track, closer, closer, NOW!

He pushed off from the ground, eyes focused on the running man, raising the sap in his right hand. The man's mouth opened wider, describing surprise with a perfect 'O', he slowed, and the killer had to adjust his trajectory, and slamming into the runner, he wrapped his left arm around him and rammed him into a tree behind him. He hadn't planned to push him into a tree. He had wanted to slam the man to the ground and whap him with the sap until he stopped moving. At least, that's how he envisioned it happening in his mind. The tree, a thick, leafless oak, acted as a brick wall and stopped them both with jarring violence. Accumulated snow dropped on them like a thick blanket, blinding the killer momentarily. When he could see again, the man's eyes were boring into him, and the man's teeth were a straight line of piano keys in his mouth.

The man said, "You messed with the wrong m-"

The killer headbutted him in the nose. Blood blossomed and he followed the headbutt with raining blows from the sap. The man crumpled to the ground, his face and head a bloody mess.

Seeing the blood on the tree and the snow, the killer thought if anyone else came along the trail now, this would be one noticeable scene of carnage. He quickly brushed snow over the area. Maybe too quickly. He hadn't noticed the earbuds the man had been wearing. The ones that had been knocked out from the impact. The possibility of discovery prohibited fine attention. Time to move.

He put the sap back into one of his many concealed pockets, picked up the feet of the man and dragged him off the trail. He used zip-ties to secure the man's hands in front, tight to his waist. Next, he bound the feet with zip-ties and used a nylon rope to link the two sets of ties together. If the man wanted to escape, he'd have to break the link first. A lesson learned from Bibi. He inserted the gag, placed duct tape over the gag and around his head. He made sure the man could breathe through his nose after the headbutt. The killer removed four separate leather straps of varying lengths with pegs on the ends. He put one strap over the forehead, and the others over his chest, pelvis and feet. He hammered the pegs into the hard earth. Now the man was completely immobilized. He put a foil warming blanket on him, covering him from head to toe. And using the white tarp he had set aside to collect falling snow, he gently pulled this tarp over the man, careful to keep as much snow on it as possible. The killer glanced at his watch and winced. A little over five minutes. When practicing this on a dummy at home, his best time had been four minutes and thirteen seconds. He was not satisfied with five minutes. Definitely too long. Oh well. It gave him something else to work on. He removed the man's cell phone from his pocket, swiped up on the locked screen, put it in airplane mode. The killer removed the SIM card, stomped on the phone until it crunched under his boot. He dug two holes in the hard dirt about ten feet apart. He put the phone in one, the SIM card in the other.

He removed a snow brush from his bag and used it to obscure the marks in the snow and cover the spots of blood he saw. He couldn't backtrack the man's steps too far, but he did enough of it that only someone looking for footprints would notice when they stopped. Which, hopefully, would be no one.

He moved back to his hiding spot and positioned himself again and got ready to settle in and wait for darkness. This was the hard part. Waiting. What if the man was expected at a certain time? What would they do if the man didn't show up? Come out to where this fool obviously ran with regularity or would they call the cops to have a look? If it was his work, would they assume he was sick and wait for him to show up the next day? If so, and work was done for the day and he didn't show up at home, did he have anyone waiting for him? All these 'what-ifs'. The reactions of the people waiting for his catches were impossible to anticipate. To do that, he'd have to know his prey beforehand and that would make the disappearances not random. Randomness equalled freedom: that was the most important facet he had to protect. The worst that could happen would be the police descending with force on this trail. And unless the police *knew* something terrible had happened, all they would do was take a report and maybe, just maybe send a patrol officer out here to check the area for the man or his car. All these counterproductive thoughts got annoying after a time because they were out of his control. All he could do was sit and wait for the night. Might as well settle in. He had food, drink, and a hole scraped out near his crotch in case he had to piss. With any luck, he'd walk out of here at night with his prize.

•   •   •

The catch woke a few hours into the killer's wait. Other than the potential of people walking by, concerned friends, or diligent cops taking notice of him, there was the added danger of his catch suffering from a concussion. He had hit the man really hard on the head numerous times. He had been aiming for the soft spot behind the man's ear and above the jaw (he'd read that was the most effective spot to use a sap on), except the man was moving when he'd hit him. In fact, the man had been in the act of turning to maybe defend himself and although the killer intended to strike that particular area, the execution of said technique was most assuredly lacking. What was one of the first things doctors warned you about when they thought you had a concussion? Vomiting. There was dizziness, blackouts, and possible memory loss, but vomiting was the most worrisome to him because the catch had a gag in his mouth. If he puked, he'd choke on it, he'd die and that would be that. And that was how his day passed. Eating a snack, sipping on coconut water, the killer intermittently checked on his catch to see if he was still breathing. He didn't want him to die on him. He had planned something special for this catch. That might be an exaggeration. All of his plans were special. This one was different though and elaborate. Most of the time, keeping it simple proved to be the best method. What did Leonardi DaVinci say? Oh yeah, 'Simplicity is the ultimate form of sophistication'. Something like that. Even though the end he had planned for this catch wasn't simple, it was sophisticated. He was pretty excited about the whole thing, to tell the truth. He hoped the man wouldn't die and wondered once again if he could get away from using the sap because of the potential for life-threatening injury.

He had started working on making his own chloroform from an ingredient list he'd found on the internet. And therein lay the problem: internet science. He could only test the concoction on himself and the one time he used it on himself, the experience scared him off trying it again.

There he was eyes already watering from the smell of the chemicals after removing the lid from the glass jar (which he should have taken as a warning). He splashed a bit onto a cloth and clamped the lid back on the jar. With the damp cloth in hand, he sat down on a loveseat, held the cloth up to his nose and... twelve hours and thirteen minutes later he woke up with the headache of all headaches. His mouth was dry, and snot coated his upper lip. He had shit his pants and pissed himself, a double whammy of disgusting. He carried a headache around for two weeks after that. Not a fun experience. That was all behind him now. This sap work was getting dangerous though. He should continue to refine his chloroform. He was a professional after all. Setbacks only provided opportunities to improve.

He checked on his catch one more time. Still breathing, no vomit anywhere. He smiled and waited for the night, his excitement and nervousness competing with each other.

•　　•　　•

This time, and every time since Bibi, he brought the catch of the day to his truck first if he couldn't also carry his gear at the same time. He consistently worked out with heavyweights because he never knew how large his catch would be. He could perform 'Farmer Walks' with one hundred and fifty pounds in each hand. He could deadlift five hundred and ten pounds and he practiced throwing beer kegs with different weights of sand in them. He stacked weights on a sled and used a heavy rope to pull it toward him with his arms. Then, with more weight added, he would use the rope to hitch himself to the sled and he would run like a sled dog. He didn't lack the strength, but the logistics of moving his catch and carrying his gear proved awkward. The problem was the lack of extra appendages. This time, he could sling the backpack on, run the straps of the duffel bag up to his arm onto his shoulder, and pull the catch in the makeshift-tarp-sled along the path back toward his truck. He twisted the straps he used to peg the man to the ground together to make a pull rope that was secured to the tarp with only the man's head peeking out of the top. He was proud of the setup. Using all the gear to secure and hide his catches, in this weather, he could use the same gear to transport his catches over the snow, obscuring his own footprints behind him. Before he started dragging the catch, he could see the rounded eyes flitting back and forth in the man's skull, the very image of fear. He smiled at the man and put on his night-vision goggles. With the night-vision goggles lowered over his eyes and powered on, the white of the snow made the night become brighter than day. Almost like he needed sunglasses from the glare the night-vision goggles created.

With his load, he trekked through the snow toward his truck, exertion exhalations in the cold air appeared like green-tinted clouds before the lenses of his goggles. He paused along the treeline and dropped to one knee. He scanned the lot. Only his truck sat there behind the closed diner. It was safe to approach. He walked to the truck without incident. He left the catch on the side of his truck farthest from the entrance to the lot, keeping his truck between the view from the road and the body on the ground. He opened the back of the truck (the interior light had been disabled), tossed his goggles over the back of the driver's headrest to land on the seat. Behind the front seats of the truck, he had a work chest, like something a contractor would have to hold their tools. He opened it and pushed the passenger seat as far forward as it would go. He lifted the catch with a grunt and shoved him into the chest. Their eyes met. Next, he put his gear on top of the catch and he closed the lid and secured the clasp on the side closest to him, right under the Snap-On logo. Time to go.

-9-

The catch, Ken Vega, knew he was in deep shit. Not only in it up to his neck, no, no, but he was also totally submerged in it, drowning in it, and what could he do about it? Trussed up like a Christmas Turkey and stuffed in a box. Man, he'd have to do some crazy Houdini magic to get out of this.

He felt like crying. Crying until his nose and eyes burned and his chest would hurt from all the hitching. He hadn't cried like that since he was a kid and his dog, a spotted white and brown retriever, named Lionel, died on their beige carpet in the living room. Ken had been kneeling on the floor, putting together a bitchin' new Star Wars Lego set with Luke Skywalker and the Rancor from *Return of the Jedi,* and Lionel was asleep on his dog mattress right under the wall hanging TV, where he had always slept. Ken had the Rancor chomping on Luke because it was his playset, right? And it got boring if the good guys *always* won, didn't it? Ken thought it'd be fun for Luke to get eaten because in the movie, it had always made him a little sad to see the Rancor's trainer crying after Luke dropped the spiked gate down on its head killing it. The Rancor had obviously meant a lot to the trainer and to see someone else kill it must have been really hard on him. Ken thought of what he was doing was saving the Rancor from Luke. He didn't think of it as killing Luke. He hadn't considered Luke at all. He only thought of the Rancor living, and to do that, Luke had to go.

As the Rancor was snarling (Ken's voice) and chomping on the plastic arm of Luke, Lionel yelped, popped up onto all fours, looked at Ken, growled, looked at his own stomach and growled again.

Ken: "Mom!"

Lionel whined, sniffed the air, focused on Ken again, wagged his tail and collapsed. A smell wafted from Lionel. A stench of poop and a rancid smell making Ken remember that time he opened the green bin lid, where all the food waste went, and wriggling on top was a party of feasting maggots. It was that sharp ammonia smell undercut with a bouquet of rotting meat. Lionel stood without realizing he moved, holding the Rancor in one hand and little Lego Luke in the other. A brackish liquid poured out of Lionel's back end, soaking his tail and the mattress. Ken burst into tears. And for a month or so after that event, every so often, in the quiet of the night, he'd remember Lionel and cry himself to sleep. Those cries were sad cries. This time, being driven somewhere in the back of a lunatic's truck, he was sad for sure but that wasn't all. Underlying the sadness for his soon-to-be-lost-life was another feeling. He knew of only one word to describe it: dread. A hollowness in the gut, a throbbing in the veins, pulsing in time with the deep bass theme from a movie such as *Jaws*. He knew there wouldn't be a happy ending for him here. The truck stopped, idled, made turns and accelerated on its way to a place, for him, was nowhere good. After some time, Ken had no idea how long they had been driving for. The truck's tires went from smooth asphalt to bouncing ruts, crunching sticks, shifting gravel and they travelled that way for once again who knew how long? And all the time, the feeling in Ken's stomach worsened. The dread deepened, feeling his heart pulse painful sludge throughout his immobilized body. Tension and pressure, building and building inside him. Ken didn't know how much more of this he could take before his mind snapped and took a break from all this. Before his brain said, *Well, nice knowing you. Time to go to away-land where none of this shit can touch me. Body of mine? You take care now and tell that crazy snowman bastard that Ken's brain told him to go fuck himself with a dildo covered in broken glass shards.* The truck stopped.

Ken heard a door open, close, and footsteps fading, receding until the only sound left was the ticking of the cooling engine. With the fabric of the gag gooey in his mouth, his thoughts raced in the silence, *I'm not ready to die yet. Not ready. I was going to ask Matt to move in with me, finally going to make the transition from casual to a serious relationship and then this, right? Of course, this.* He thought more of Matt and where he was right now and what he might be doing. He was at a conference, an Archeology one. A topic that immediately acted as a sedative on Ken whenever Matt mentioned his work and what new theories were being discussed, disputed and dissected. Matt was probably in his hotel room right now, reading incredibly boring historical nonsense while *Breaking Bad* streamed on the TV in the background. Matt loved that show, had watched it over and over again and liked to have it on as background noise while he worked. And now here Ken was in the back of a psycho's truck, and let's face it, he was going to be killed. What a total waste.

The door popped open, and the lid of the chest raised. There was the man again wearing a white mask in a white hood. Ken experienced a full-bodied violent shiver.

"I'm going to take your gag off. You'll be tempted to scream, and you're more than welcome to. No one will hear you, but I don't expect you to take my word for it. If I was in your shoes, I wouldn't either. BUT, and that's a but with a capital 'B', when I ask you to stop because squealing like that, after a time, tends to get on my nerves, you better stop. And I mean right quick."

The man in white raised a knife, pointed it at Ken and said, "Nod if you understand me."

Ken nodded.

The knife disappeared and the man in white reached in, removed the gag straps tape and said, "You can spit it out now. I don't want to touch it."

Ken pushed the gag out with his tongue. He dry-heaved when it was halfway out, and he spit out the rest of it onto his chest. He stared at the man in white.

"You not going to scream?"

"No."

"Huh. Okay then."

The man in white reached into the tool chest, pulled Ken's legs up and out, and said, "This part is going to be rough. It's a lot harder to wrestle you out than it is to put you in there. Expect some pain."

With that said, the man in white grunted, pulled, and twisted Ken out of the chest and placed him with surprising gentleness on the ground.

Ken said, "You know, you could cut the end of the chest there, so it would drop down like a little bridge. Be easy to get someone out then. Just slide them along."

The man in white stared at Ken. He said, "That is a good idea. I don't know why I didn't think of that. You know, you're really calm for someone in your position. The calmest person I've had so far."

The calmest person I've had so far... Ken blinked as he absorbed that statement. His heart thudded. Snow started to drop out of the night sky, fat lazy flakes, floating drops of white reflecting the moon's rays. A beautiful night. If it wasn't for the situation he was in, he knew he wouldn't have noticed such a night. Normally at this time he'd be in bed after stretching and a shower and would be thinking about calling Matt or waiting for Matt to call him. Right now, in this situation though, he noticed everything.

He swallowed and said, "You're going to kill me, aren't you?"

"Yeah. I told you as much earlier with my little speech in the woods, didn't I?"

"Yeah, you did." Ken opened his mouth, caught some snow on his tongue. Cold. A pleasant cold.

Ken said, "Is it going to be bad?"

"Yeah."

Ken started crying. He didn't want to. The night was so pretty, he just couldn't help himself.

•　　•　　•

The man in white dragged Ken by his feet toward a hole in the ground. Beside this hole was a keg or something, a big container with a hose coiled up in the snow. He furrowed his brow, wondering what the hell was that all about until he saw the shape of the hole and worse, what was in it. A big, person-sized rectangular hole, with a big, person-sized rectangular box in it. *Let's be real here, it's not a box, it's a coffin! He's going to put you in that fucking coffin!*

Ken said, "No, no, no, no-" and he tried turning, twisting his torso, pulling his legs in but the man in white kept walking. The distance from the truck to the hole, the coffin, wasn't far after all and it took no time at all, really, to end up before the coffin and after a hard yank from the man in white, he dropped into the box.

"Look at that. A perfect fit."

Ken crunched up into a seated position. The man in white kicked him in the center of his chest with his heavy boot. Ken fell back. Tremendous pain twisted his features. Spit and snot shot out of his mouth and nose, and before he could raise himself again, the thick plywood lid slammed down on him, striking his forehead. Dancing firefly lights moved behind his eyelids.

Ken said, "No!" and pushed against the inside of the lid with his hands but the man in white had tied his arms tight to his body and he could generate no force because of that. A power drill sounded, and Ken heard the screws biting into the wood.

"NO! Stop! Please stop! Please! Oh please, fuck, no, no, no!"

Ken continued to scream and plead to the underside of the lid as it was screwed to the coffin he found himself in. He couldn't stop himself. He said he wouldn't scream when the gag was taken off, but he didn't know this was going to happen. He knew something terrible was planned for him, but this? Who could guess something like this would happen? That something like this could happen to anyone outside of a novel or a scary movie? It was something that would never have occurred to him. His brain felt scrambled. Like someone had cut the top part of his skull off, took a big wooden spoon, and started spinning the grey matter around and around. He couldn't focus, he could only scream and plead to the man whom he knew wasn't listening. If he could calm down, he might have noticed the coffin was lined with plastic. A swishing noise accompanied his frantic movements. That would have made him think, why the plastic? And he might have thought about the container and the hose. But there was no time for calm. Especially when the sounds of the drilling stopped and the sounds of earth hitting the top of the coffin began. Ken screamed his voice raw.

-10-

There were two containers actually, both filled with water and the appropriate amount of antifreeze with two hoses connected to them. Those containers had been a bitch to get out of his truck. He had a dolly for that reason but pulling the containers of water over the rough ground was still a pain in the ass. In the end, he hoped it'd be worth it. The two hoses ran into the ground and one entered the coffin by the shoulder and the other by the feet. He sealed the coffin with plastic and used caulking to seal where the hoses entered the coffin. When he thought up this plan of disposal, he initially thought he was so clever. Kill the person in an inventive way, in an out-of-the-way place, and they were already buried and hidden. There'd still be more clean-up to do by the end, sure, but most of it would be done at the end of the killing. The only trouble was, he liked to watch. He liked seeing their fear. He liked seeing their helplessness. What he liked to see (loved was a more accurate word for it), was their life leaving them. The soul, the id, the electrical pulses, whatever you want to call it, the thing that animates the body, when that left, when that faded from their eyes… whoa. There was nothing in this world like it. And being the cause of it? It was god-like. So, how to do this fun and creative way to murder someone and be able to watch it happen? He'd need a camera.

What he needed was a small camera with night vision capabilities that wasn't traceable to any of his identities through a unique purchase. It'd have to be easily accessible to everyone. Where to get a camera that anyone can buy and not be suspicious while doing so? Amazon of course. A quick search yielded what he wanted. A micro camera, no larger than his pinky, with Blu-tooth connectivity to his phone. The only hitch was, he couldn't get it with night vision. He'd have to use a small remote light. Charge them both up, sync them to his phone and he was ready to go. All of this amazing technology, cheap, and anonymous, delivered to a PO Box to help him with his hobby of murder.

After he covered the coffin with a layer of dirt, he checked to see if he was connected to the camera in the coffin. Check. Connection established. To the light? Yup. Connection established.

Using a burner phone just for this purpose, he turned on the remote light. Ah. There he was. Ken in all his terrified glory. Ken paused, looking like a teenager who had been caught beating off by his mom, wearing that same terrified, frozen expression. Seeing the angle now, he wished he had placed the camera in a better position. He saw one eye, the nose and the mouth from maybe six inches away. It'd have been better if he could see both eyes, like a top-down view, but that would have been too tricky and if Ken noticed it, he might be able to jar it loose with his head. And that wouldn't be good. He'd just have to be happy with what he had.

He released the valves on both of the hoses. He heard the water moving through the hose and when the cold liquid reached Ken, he jumped on the screen.

The killer said, "Showtime."

-11-

When the light came on in the coffin, Ken froze. A soft yellow glow from over his right shoulder. He could see his own chest and his hands resting below his breastbone. A black wire eye cast a shadow from underneath the coffin lid.

"What is-"

Cold water rushed in. It touched his shoulders first, his calves second. The water rose quickly.

"Hey! Hey! C'mon! Let me out! Goddamn it, let me out of here, I swear I'll be a good boy, I swear, I swear-"

Ken carried on that way, begging and pleading until the water entered his nose, his mouth and all that escaped him were bubbles. In time, those stopped too.

-12-

At around the same time Ken's coffin was filling up with water and antifreeze, Matt was sitting on his hotel room bed, legs out before him, back propped against the headboard, reading Graham Hancock's book, *America Before, The Key To Earth's Lost Civilization*, with *Breaking Bad* playing on the TV as background noise. Graham Hancock's books were a guilty pleasure of Matt's and if anyone of his peers in the Archeology world knew about this particular pleasure, he risked ostracization. Graham Hancock was openly critical of Archeologists and what he saw as their stubborn adherence to doctrine despite intriguing evidence. Even though Matt was of the archeological world, he thought Graham's work was fun, if not a little biased as he tended to overvalue the vague clues of the past. On the side table sat a glass of Limoncello within easy reach and beside that was his cell phone. Normally, after a long day of networking and listening to presentations, reading Graham's book would be a nice end to his day. This evening, however, he was having trouble focusing. Ken had not called him all day. Even worse than that, Ken hadn't answered his phone at all when Matt tried to call him.

Matt had expected a call early this morning after Ken finished his morning run. When they weren't together, Ken always called after a run, just to say hi, catch up or to make plans later in the evening. It was one of the things that they did. Like arguing, no, discussing, baseball and whose team would do better. Ken was a diehard Toronto Blue Jays fan and Matt was a devoted Boston Red Sox fan and they both knew their team players and their stats and could rhyme them off without consulting the sports page or the internet. The best evenings were when the two teams faced each other. Ken in a Blue Jay jersey and hat, and Matt in a Red Sox T-shirt and a hat, watching the game with beer, chips, and wings on the table. The night of the last game in the series usually (if their arguments, no, discussions didn't get too heated) ended in a little both-lightly-drunk bit of loving. A perfect end to a fun evening.

Matt closed the book and put it on his lap. He picked up his cell phone and the face glowed. He chewed on his lip. No texts. No missed calls.

"Fuck it."

Matt dialled Ken's number. The voicemail clicked, Ken's voice said, *Too busy to answer right now, if it's really important, leave a message.* Beep.

"Hey Ken. Call me back. I'm getting a little worried here."

He clicked the red end button. He chewed his lip again. He was getting worried which was strange for him because he wasn't the worrying type. But there it was, a tingle below his belly button. The patter of ant feet under his skin. Matt was good at recognizing patterns. It could be he was good at them because of his training or it could be he was good at them because he liked puzzles and puzzle solving was all about pattern recognition. This pattern he was detecting was a broken one. When they were apart, Ken would phone twice a day without fail. Once after his morning run on the same trail he always ran, rain, shine, snow, muck, didn't matter, Ken always ran, and he always called after he ran. The second time Ken would always call (there that word is again, always) was later in the evening, between 7pm and 9pm to say, goodnight, I love you, I'll call you in the morning. It was past 9pm now and Ken hadn't called him once.

The ants under his skin got even busier. What to do about it? What could he do about it?

His feet twitched from side to side. Janelle!

He dialled Janelle's number.

"Hello?"

"Janelle? Matt here, I wonder if you could do me a big favour?"

•   •   •

Janelle lived next door to Matt. They had a neighbourly agreement in which if one of them happened to be out of town, the other would watch their home, water plants, and in Janelle's case, Matt would feed her cat. Over time they became friends and spent many a summer evening together barbequing, drinking, and talking. Janelle lived alone, dated often, but wasn't, in her own opinion, the marrying type. Her relationships usually dissolved when the man in her life finally realized that yup, she meant it, she really didn't want to get married or have kids, and that would be that. Her and Matt were good friends, bordering on great friends which was why Matt had no trouble calling her to ask her if she would drive over to Ken's to see if he was home.

"Yeah, I can do that. Is everything all right with you two? Like, am I checking up on him for maybe a trust issue?"

"No, no. I'm worried, that's all. He always calls me, and he hasn't once today and he's not answering his phone and it's night now... I just want to make sure he's okay."

"All right. I'll call you when I get over there."

"Thanks."

"Don't mention it. You know I like Ken. Almost more than I like you. If you're worried, then I'm worried."

"Okay."

•   •   •

Janelle drove through a white tunnel of falling snow. Every year, she had her snow tires installed and with how slick the roads felt, she was glad she had done so this snowy evening. Her wipers wiped, and the radio played Micheal Jackson's *Wanna Be Startin' Something,* and before the song finished, she stopped before Ken's condo staring at Ken's empty parking spot. Twinkling lights lined balconies in chains of white celebrating a Christmas that had yet to arrive. Janelle drove through the whole lot to make sure he hadn't parked anywhere else. Ken's car was not on the property.

Janelle called Matt.

"His car's not here."

"No?"

"It's not in his spot and I don't see it anywhere else in the lot here."

"Damnit!"

"If you're that worried, and it seems like you are, maybe you should call the police."

"Yeah, yeah, but can you check one more spot for me before I do that?"

"Of course."

"Every morning, Ken goes running on the trail, I uh forget the name-"

"Oren Reid?"

"Yeah. That's the one. How'd you know that?"

"I remember you making fun of Ken having to leave a party or something pretty early so he could get up the next morning to go running on that trail."

"Jeez, that was a long time ago."

"I remember weird things."

"Ok, so he parks where the trail crosses Alice Street, a bit west of Dakota Drive."

"Yup. I know where that is. What are you thinking?"

"I'm thinking, like the lunatic he is, he went running on the trail in the morning darkness. He might have hurt himself. God, I hope he didn't hurt himself."

"I'll head over there now, and I'll call you when I get there."

"Thanks, Janelle. Really."

"Hey, c'mon. Wouldn't you do the same for me? If I had a significant other or even just an other?"

"Yeah."

"Shut up about it then."

• • •

Janelle saw the car, a dark Tesla, with a generous layer of snow on it.

She said, "Oh no."

She parked beside it, rolled down her window. There were no footprints running away from the car or toward it.

With a dry mouth, she called Matt. She dreaded telling him what she had found. She worried for her friend. For both of them.

-13-

Although the trail ran around the Region of Waterloo, the area itself was the responsibility of the Ontario Provincial Police. Matt called them and spoke with dispatch, who connected him with the station closest to the Oren Reid trail. Matt spoke with the front desk constable, and not liking the lack of urgency in the police officer's voice, demanded to speak with a supervisor.

"Hello, this is Sergeant MacKenzie."

Matt explained to the Sergeant the reason for the late-night call. Sergeant MacKenzie listened to the measured voice on the line, detailing in a calm, factual manner, why the matter of his missing boyfriend Ken deserved the police's immediate attention. Under the calmness, Sergeant MacKenzie heard a quavering, almost pleading sound, like a man hanging onto the edge of a balcony by his fingertips, forty stories high, hoping someone would reach down and help him up. After hearing everything, the Sergeant agreed that there was a reason for concern, and he would send what resources he had available to the area to see if they could find Ken.

The relief was palpable in Matt's voice.

Sergeant MacKenzie: "What is the best way to reach you?"

"My cell phone. I'm going to get a rental car right now and make my way home."

"It might be best to make that drive home in the morning. We are going to get snow off and on all night, and if you're tired, that's not a good combination."

"I'll be worse in the morning. I won't be able to sleep until I know he's okay."

"Yeah. Drive careful then. I'll call you as soon as we know something."

"Okay. Thank you."

Sergeant MacKenzie checked the roster of available officers. A K-9 officer was in his area tonight. She had been used to execute a warrant nearby, but the warrant was done, and she still had two hours to go in her shift. Well, that was handy. And unusually lucky for him. K-9 officers were notoriously hard to get a hold of. Specialty units all over the province used them, and there wasn't a whole lot of them to begin with. Might be a good idea to buy a lottery ticket with that kind of luck.

Sergeant MacKenzie called dispatch and arranged for the K-9 officer and two road constables to go to the trail and search for Ken.

-14-

The standard procedure for when a K-9 officer was working a track was for another officer to assist them. The reason being the K-9 handler paid attention to their dog. The dog's tail would swish, or the dog might go still or display varied responses during the track that only the handler, having spent time with the dog since it was a puppy, would be able to interpret. Now, if the handler happened to be tracking a dangerous person, the handler wouldn't be able to watch the dog and be aware of their surroundings. They might walk into an ambush. The second officer was meant to guard the handler. And because the handler was usually a fit person (they wouldn't last long in the unit if they weren't), the second officer with them should also be someone who was in good physical shape and could keep up with them. Junior officers, newbies, fresh from the Ontario Police College, were, by and large, in good shape. The K-9 officer was the last to arrive at the Tesla. When she arrived, she saw two overweight men who appeared to be playing rock-paper-scissors. She smiled, parked next to a police cruiser, and stepped out.

"Who lost?"

"Don't know yet. Best seven out of ten."

She let her dog out and he bounded to her, nuzzled her hand, and she said, "Ready to work Gerrold?"

He chuffed at her.

"Damn it! Best seventeen out of twenty?"

"No. You lost. You run. I'll stand here and guard the cruisers from, you know, thieves."

The officer who lost lifted the police toque from his forehead and scratched at the thinning hair underneath. He turned to face the K-9 officer and when he did, he smiled. It made him look younger, despite the thinning hair.

"Oh. Hey Cheryl. How you been?"

"Ted? Man, how long has it been?"

He rubbed his belly overtop his vest and said, "About twenty-eight pounds ago."

She laughed and said, "How are the little ones?"

"Not so little anymore. The oldest, she's going to Queen's University."

"Wow! When did that happen? What does she want to do?"

He shrugged, "I don't know. Find herself, I guess."

"An expensive way to do that."

"You're not kidding."

"You ready?"

"Nope. But let's get it done anyway."

Cheryl noticed the other officer sitting in his cruiser, sipping on a coffee. Not the sociable type, she guessed.

• • •

Nighttime tracking presented its own set of unique problems. Sight being the most obvious and challenging one. Running while keeping track of the dog, holding a flashlight in one hand, updating dispatch over the portable radio on the shoulder with the other while trying not to step into a gopher hole, erosion dips, tripping on roots, and avoiding sharp, raking branches, made nighttime tracking more difficult than any other time of tracking. On a winter night, with fresh snowfall, and the moon reflecting the soft crystalline flakes, sight was less of an issue. Gerrold wore a reflective police vest and even though Cheryl didn't need her flashlight, she still used it for areas where shadows collected under trees. She followed tracks, older ones as the snow had filled them partway and the edges were softer, as though someone smoothed them out with a hand. Gerrold moved ahead, nose ploughing a furrow, at a steady pace. They weren't running, which would have been challenging in the shin-deep snow, even still, she heard Ted breathing hard a few feet behind her, taking big gulps of air with every step. She looked back, concerned, and Ted waved her forward. Cheryl nodded and kept pace with Gerrold until the footprints disappeared.

She frowned, shining her light on the ground to see if she missed them somehow, or maybe Gerrold had destroyed them while tracking. Behind her,

Ted gasped for air. She could smell him, smell his sweat and his coffee breath exhales into the back of her neck.

She fanned the flashlight beam in an arc. Where did the prints go? Unless the person floated up into the sky, there should be more prints here. Were they brushed away? Her mind focused, sharpened. The stakes had risen.

"What's", breath, "the hold-up?"

"The footprints, they're gone."

"Wind?"

"No. To get through the trees, it'd have to be a strong wind and even then, all the prints would be gone. They wouldn't just stop like this... in a line."

"What does it mean?"

BARK!

Cheryl flicked the light to Gerrold. He pointed his nose at a spot near the base of a tree. His body posture and the stillness of it...

"He's found something."

Cheryl studied the ground before moving. She didn't want to mess up potential evidence and walked wide of where the footprints would have been if they still existed.

"Stay behind me."

This wasn't Ted's first time at a potential scene. He didn't question her. He followed her lead.

Cheryl stopped behind Gerrold and shone her light where his snout was pointed. She bent down into a squat and using her gloved hand, she moved the snow away from where Gerrold's nose had pressed in. She took her time. She had worked as a Scenes of Crime Officer and knew slow, meticulous movement was best. Push, dig, push and there, an Apple AirPods, something a runner would wear to listen to music. On the AirPod, was that a bit of scarlet there?

Cheryl said, "Shit."

Ted, leaning over her shoulder and seeing what Cheryl was seeing said, "Fuck me. Here comes a crap night of unwanted overtime."

In the bright light of the flashlight, a blood coated AirPod sat.

Cheryl said, "Better call Crime Scene and Investigative Services. Sooner rather than later."

Still winded from his brief run, Ted said, "Yeah."

• • •

They found blood on a tree, a crushed cell phone in one spot and a SIM card not too far away. In another place were the vague outlines of two people, lying down. It was delicate work protecting a scene in the snow. They had lights to brighten up the area, but they didn't want it to melt any of the snow before photos of any tracks could be obtained. Once that was done, they concentrated on the areas where they thought the people had lain, searching for anything tangible, any evidence that would not melt. There were plenty of crime scene technicians in the area. At the outset, this incident appeared to be an abduction, a major case. Investigators were called out in the middle of the night to interview Matt and compile a list of people who had known Ken. What did Ken do for a living? Did he have enemies? Did his job place him at high risk for violence? Detective-Sergeant (D/S) Moulton was one of the investigators called out.

A track of something (a person?) was followed to the parking lot behind an out-of-business diner from the area where two human shapes marred the snow. Tire tracks, barely discernible, were photographed. Sergeant MacKenzie called Matt and told him what they knew. As expected, Matt did not take the information well. Sergeant MacKenzie contacted Victim Services on behalf of Matt. Then, as directed by D/S Moulton, Sergeant MacKenzie prepared a media release statement to make the public aware of the incident and to enlist their help. Not that he expected any witnesses to an event in a remote area, but it never hurt to ask.

-15-

When Ken was already in the custody of the killer, lying under a tarp off the running trail about four hundred feet away, Parmajit Singh listened to the radio in her car with her camera on the seat beside her following the directions on her phone. Parmajit (Parm to her friends) headed to Louise's Eggstravaganza to take photos for her real estate listing. It would be a less than lucrative assignment, but she was the new person in the REMAX office, and the new listings, the ones the managers thought would take a long time to move, went to the newbies.

When she turned off the highway, she didn't see the pickup truck at first because it had been parked behind the building. She parked out front and scanned the front of the diner through the windshield of her car, planning her photos. What marketing pitch could she use to sell this dump? Enjoy this out of business diner in this remote location during COVID. No one was leaving their homes, afraid to do so, which was why this place was closed and was now available for you to purchase to have your dreams of opening a restaurant crash and burn under an economic boulder only billionaires could hope to move! She blew irritation out of her nostrils. What would she even list the price at?

She picked up her camera, turned off her car, and stepped out into the brisk air. She snapped a few photos thinking the sun in the cold air made the colours crisper, more vibrant. She walked around the building and saw the truck. An ugly machine tucked tight against the treeline. It occurred to her that maybe the truck had been abandoned or maybe even stolen and then abandoned. Not her problem. To make this diner look less pathetic, less lonesome, she thought it might be good to include it in a couple of her pictures. She walked to the far side of it and took some photos with it in the foreground of the diner. Not bad. Not great, but what more could she do to try to sell this loser of a building?

The next morning, she saw the request for help by the police on her Twitter feed. She followed the Waterloo Regional Police Service, the Guelph Police

Service, and the Ontario Provincial Police on Twitter. They sometimes gave traffic updates, letting the public know what roads were closed due to accidents and she generally liked to know what was going on in the area. The title read, MAN TAKEN FROM TRAIL, WITNESSES URGED TO COME FORWARD. She clicked the link, saw where the man had gone missing from, said, "I was right there!"

"What's that mom?" Her son, pausing with a spoonful of cereal lifted to his mouth, asked her.

"Nothing," she said while reading the rest of the short news release.

Parm didn't call the police right then. She spent the morning getting her children ready for school and drinking steaming cups of coffee. Her mind kept returning to the diner and to the pick-up truck. She should call the police, just in case. She felt a little stupid though. She hadn't actually witnessed anything, did she? All she did was take a picture of a pick-up truck. What was that worth? Better let them decide.

-16-

Bibi saw the image of the pick-up truck on the TV. She'd been having lunch with Rori, at a sports bar with TVs lining every wall, covering the windows, and reflecting onto shiny bar tops. Bibi liked the poutine here. They used real gravy. Gravy so thick she could eat it with a fork. Maybe not quite that thick, but thick enough with a rich meaty flavour, and hot enough to melt the cheese curds into a beautiful tongue-stinging mess. Rori had a salad, because that's what she always ate and only when she was feeling particularly peckish would she add a BLT sandwich on the side. No BLT today for Rori, just a kale salad with chunks of foul-smelling blue cheese sprinkled on top. Rori had been regaling Bibi with a tale of her boyfriend, Pete, from last night. In the middle of the night, he'd gotten up to use the washroom, his naked sun-deprived ass shined in the moonlight from the window, and for whatever reason, Rori had left a plastic bag on the floor of the room which ended up providing a scene straight out of a slapstick comedy.

"You know, I wake up pretty easy. And when his weight left the bed, I woke up," Rori sipped from her glass, continued, "with one eye cracked, watching him cross the room. I heard the bag, that rustling, crinkling, plastic bag sound, and I don't know how he did it, but," she covered her mouth as she giggled, "but, one foot must have got stuck in the handle part as he stepped on the back part and when he lifted his foot like you would when, you know, walking forward, he tripped and his junk? It hit the end of the bed, the wooden part, as he fell, and I don't think I'd ever heard a sound like that before coming from a person's mouth." She laughed, covering her mouth, but Bibi wasn't laughing.

Bibi's eyes were transfixed to a position over Rori's shoulder. On the screen was a photo of a pick-up truck in front of a restaurant, diner, what it was didn't matter, only that pick-up truck sure mattered. The image made Bibi think of a hike through the woods, of a man rising from the earth, hands and legs bound, and the darkness of a damp hole in the ground. A sky-blue truck, rust over the one visible wheel well, and on the back window, a MEC sticker.

"Bibi. What's wrong? Are you ok?"

The words were muffled, almost silent, as though they travelled to her ears underwater. Bibi felt the sweat on her brow and that confused her. It was contrary to the cold, icy feeling emanating from the very center of her.

There was a phone number on the screen below the image. Bibi blinked, raised her phone, and snapped a photo of the screen capturing the phone number at the bottom. Without answering Rori or even looking at her, she stood, said, "Sorry, I have to go," and rushed out of the restaurant.

-17-
EDUCATION PART 5

After a year, the killer had earned a six percent return. He showed the figures to his father.

"That's not bad. I might have gotten eight percent, might have, still, six percent is acceptable."

The only time his father ever approached normalcy was when talking about investing or the creation of multiple identities. Within the last year, his father showered less and less and would wear the same clothes for weeks at a time. He sent the killer out to hunt on his own for their meat. Considering how much money they had, he thought it ludicrous not to buy all their food and have it delivered to them. He showed his father a subscription food service where they'd replenish your food weekly if you wanted them to and his father glared at him and said, "I don't want people coming here. And I don't want any regular credit card charges. Have I taught you nothing, boy? You hunt for our meat and you get our other groceries the same way we have always done it. At different stores, in different towns, paying in cash."

Staring at the computer screen, his father's unbrushed mouth exhaled garlic, and for some reason the scent of dirt, he said, "Yeah. Solid work there. Now, I'll show you how to spread the money around to different identities. If you have too much in one place, the government will want more of a piece. Greedy motherfuckers can never get enough. Unless it's from one of their rich friends. Those people they leave alone. They only pick on the people without the money to defend themselves. Have you read A PEOPLE'S HISTORY OF THE UNITED STATES yet?"

"Yeah."

"Then you know what I'm talking about."

"I do."

His father straightened, looked out the window, shivered, and stumbled to the kitchen. The killer wondered how much more did he need to learn from this man? From his ever-

expanding topics of reading, according to the DSM-5 (Diagnostic and Statistical Manual of Mental Disorders), he was confident his father suffered from bipolar disorder and paranoid schizophrenia. Putting him out of his misery would be a mercy.

• • •

The killer saw the same image and phone number on the TV while at home, eating a grilled cheese sandwich with ketchup (because only crazy people eat it without ketchup), a pickle and a coffee. He noticed the image did not display a licence plate. He read the scrolling words on the bottom, the police asking anyone with information about the owner of the truck, or the truck owner themselves to come forward as they may have been a witness to an abduction. Hmmm… it might have been smarter of them to keep that information as hold back evidence.

He dipped an end of his grilled cheese into the ketchup and took a bite. He took a sip of the coffee. Reading that, he took it to mean the police didn't know who owned the truck and that they didn't get a licence plate for it. The truck wasn't registered to him, so even if they had a plate, they wouldn't be knocking on his door anytime soon. To find the registered owner, they'd have to visit the Cheltenham graveyard, find the tombstone with the name Kyle Houghton, and stomp on the dirt to see if he'd answer. He'd bought the truck at auction years and years ago. He never changed the ownership for it. For what he used the truck for, he didn't think that'd be the best idea.

He continued eating, musing on the problem. He only took the truck out for his hunting excursions, maybe three or four times a year, in the early morning hours, in the darkness before the dawn. Who could have seen him? The closest neighbour was a kilometre away. They could have seen the truck as they were farmers and as such, are known as a group to be early risers. He'd have to have been really unlucky for a neighbour to have seen his truck and recognized it as belonging to him. For the rest of the time, he'd kept it in his detached garage/workshop. Realistically, he had no control over who had seen his truck and whether they could attribute the vehicle to him. What he did control was what to do with the truck now. He liked the damn thing. They had been on many adventures together and he had made many modifications to it to better contain, restrain and transport his catches. He had planned for this contingency and knew what to do, but it really annoyed him knowing he'd have to get rid of it. He took great pains, planned with great detail to position himself and his truck in a place unnoticed, where it would either blend into the background or not be seen at all. A random photo had done his truck in. He finished off the grilled cheese sandwich, washed the plate and utensils and placed them where they belonged. Everything in its place.

Above the sink, the window gave him a view of the garage/workshop. He'd get rid of the truck tonight.

-18-

A farmer *had* seen his truck. Not in the way the killer had anticipated or expected. Still, it had been seen and, unlucky for him, remembered. Their small town of Mono Mills was predominately a farming community. People out here voted conservative, went to church occasionally, and in times of need, looked after each other. This care for one's neighbours' attitude was how Nancy Thompson became involved in the killer's life. Nancy Thompson, sitting in her living room, holding a hot cup of tea in two hands, the steam fogging her glasses and the scent of peppermint invading her nostrils, watched the evening news unfold before her. The image of the truck flashed on the screen. She frowned, squinted, and said, "I know that truck. Now, why do I know that truck?"

Her husband, Johnny (even as a forty-two-year-old man, people who knew him still called him Johnny) said, "What's that?"

"How do I know that truck?"

"What truck?"

"The one right on the screen there, not five feet away from you."

"I don't know how you know what you know. I never did." He dismissed her and the conversation by returning to his Triathlon magazine. He was at that point in his life where he thought he was missing out on something, some life experience that would mean more to him than the drudgery and repetition of his farming life. And he wanted something to buy. These bikes, made of carbon fibre everything, looked fast and expensive and it felt to be the one thing he was missing in his life. And with the questioning looks Nancy gave him when he bought the magazine, he thought he might be on the right track.

"That's it! I remember."

Without looking up from his magazine, he said, "Congratulations."

"Remember that tornado warning they broadcast? Supposed to run through our town?"

He sighed, knowing he wouldn't get out of this conversation until she released him from it. He turned over the magazine, placed it on his lap, and said, "The one that touched down over by the Xanthos' farm? Yeah. I remember that. About the scariest thing I'd ever seen. And you made me stop at the neighbours there, the one we don't know. The one no one seems to know, I might add."

"Yeah. And-"

"Why'd you do that foolishness, again?"

"He's the only one not on the CB Radio band around here. Unless he was watching or listening to the weather channel, he wouldn't know he was about to be lifted to the land of OZ."

"Yeah, okay. I remember you putting our lives at risk for a stranger."

"Not a stranger. A neighbour."

"A neighbour we've never met and who has never had any interest in meeting us? That my dear, Nancy, is a stranger. How do you even know this 'neighbour' is a 'he'?"

"I saw him once, picking up trash some passing car must have tossed onto his driveway."

"About the truck?"

"Tornado day, while we were fleeing, I made you stop at his house. I wanted to make sure, is all, that if he was home, he knew it'd be a good idea to leave like we were. I knocked on his door, no answer, but with the wind blowing the way it was, I don't know how likely it would have been that he heard me. I looked in the windows, rapped on them, same as the back door, and nothing. You were honking the horn, impatient as usual, the wind was picking up, but I had to check the garage, to make sure he wasn't inside working on something with headphones on. You know, kind of like you when you're riding the tractor."

"Yeah, yeah."

"So, I knocked on the door, banged on it so hard I hurt my hand, it was sore for a week, and I peeked in the window and that's it. That's where I saw the truck."

Sensing the story was almost done, he picked up his magazine and said, "What are you going to do about it?"

"Call the police, I suppose. Or should I call on the neighbour?"

"What? And let him know you once snooped around his garage?"

"It wasn't snooping."

"Sure. But if you're going to do anything, call the police. You can remain anonymous if you want, so the neighbour never finds out about your not-snooping."

"Stop saying 'snooping'! You know I wasn't snooping."

"If you say so."

"You can be such a jerk sometimes."

"I'm not unique in that, my dear."

Nancy finished her tea. After the news, she watched TOO HOT TO HANDLE on Netflix, and completely forgot about the truck and the police. She remembered the next morning when she saw the Triathlon magazine on the counter by the coffee maker, which brought the conversation from the previous evening back to her. After breakfast, she called the police. By that time, the killer had rid himself of the truck.

-19-

Detective Sergeant Davis arrived at work, said hi to his team in the outer office before entering his own while balancing a paper bag with a bagel on his takeout coffee cup so he could unlock his office door. He stepped in, placed his food and his drink on his desk, and when his buttocks shadowed the seat of his chair, his phone rang.

Davis said, "Already?"

He sat, picked up the phone and said, "Detective Sergeant Davis of the Criminal Investigation Branch. How can I help you?"

"Missing persons is transferring that investigation to your office. You have more experience in these matters. It fits the Major Case model."

"Ok. What investigation? What are we talking about here?"

"That guy abducted from the trail? It's been all over the news..."

"I don't have cable."

"I didn't know that was a thing. A person not having cable. Do you watch TV?"

"Yeah. I stream."

"Oh. Ok. I must be getting old."

No answer.

"Anyway, it never should have gone to missing persons. The guy's not missing. He was taken. The evidence suggests that."

"Can you give me a basic run down? I really have no idea what you're talking about."

"Ok. Guy goes for a run, is taken from the trail. We have bloody earbuds, a crushed phone, a SIM card, and drag marks from the area of the earbuds and phone to a nearby parking lot. We got a picture of a vehicle that was there on the day of the abduction, and when we enter the particulars of the vehicle into the MCM database, we get a hit to an attempt abduction from around five years ago. Right around the time the Jackal case was nearing the end."

"You already got a hit from MCM?"

MCM or Major Case Management is a database that all police services in Ontario use for particular offences. All the information for what is deemed a major case is entered and if there are similar incidents that have occurred in Ontario, the investigator will be notified and will have more investigative leads to follow. The database was created after the Bernardo/Homolka rapes and murders. Paul Bernardo's name as a suspect had been written down four times but since there had been over ten thousand tips to go through, it hadn't been noticed. He was also raping women in different cities. If they had the Major Case Database then, Bernardo would have been caught a lot earlier. The database might have saved lives. After that case, the Major Case Management was developed, and the Ontario government forced implementation on all the police services.

"Well, we had help. The victim of the attempt abduction called us and was adamant that was the truck she had seen. Did I mention it was from five years ago?"

"Yeah, you did." Davis sat up in his chair. Interesting.

"And this morning we got a call from a woman, a farmer up in Mono Mills, who said she is sure the owner of that truck happens to be her neighbour."

"Really? We got a file on this guy?"

"All of this should be in the case file, in the database. You can pull it up on your computer."

"Ok. I'll get on it."

"Get your team together. Keep me updated. This could get hot."

"Will do."

Davis hung up the phone. He brought up the case file and began reading what they had on the Ken Vega abduction and what they had on the Bibi Khan attempted abduction.

-20-

The Major Case Management model consisted of a lead investigator, a file coordinator, and the case manager. Davis would be the lead investigator. He'd assign one of his guys as the file coordinator, and Inspector Carlisle would manage or oversee it all. Davis' primary role was to direct other officers to follow and complete the tasks the major case program created as more and more information was entered. For now, he'd build his team, and have every one of them become familiar with the investigative information accumulated so far. He stood, closed his eyes, and pushed air out through his nose. He had a feeling about this one. The problem was, he didn't believe in feelings or directions from his gut either. He knew the feeling stemmed from his unconscious mind assembling all the information he'd just read and combined with his years of experience, he knew the two incidents, five years apart, were committed by the same person. And that meant, to his conscious mind at least, that there were more victims. Unknown victims. How many people went missing in provincial parks? Or the woods? Or hiking trails? He twisted his head to the side until his neck cracked. He had a lot of work to do.

●　　　●　　　●

He left his office and walked into a conversation taking place amongst the pool of detectives at their desks.

Stacy: "This book, it's called Unlucky Numbers?"

Gurpreet: "Yeah, yeah."

Stacy: "And the people in it win the lottery? How's that unlucky?"

Brandon: "They win, yeah, but the government doesn't want to pay them, right? They don't have the money. So, get this; they kill them!"

Stacy leaned forward in her chair, "Who kills them? The government?"

Brandon: "Yeah! That way, they don't have to pay them, and they get to keep the money!"

Gurpreet: "Yeah. Crazy, huh? Great book."

Cam stepped into the office, carrying a cardboard tray filled with coffee as it was his turn to make the daily run. He caught the end of Gurpreet's sentence, and putting the tray down on his desk, he said, "Unlucky Numbers?"

Brandon: "Yeah."

Cameron: "Great book, man."

Gurpreet: "You know it."

Stacy: "Wait, wait, wait. Let me get this straight. If the people who win the lottery keep dying, then why do people keep buying the tickets? And what about these people who win? Don't they have any family? Wouldn't the money go to them?"

Brandon, shaking his head said, "It's not that simple. You have to read the book to understand."

Gurpreet: "Yeah, read the book. You'll see."

Stacy: "Um, I'll pass on that one. Thanks though."

Davis: "Yeah. I'll pass on that too. Listen up, we got a major case assignment."

Gurpreet: "Is it the trail runner?"

Davis: "Am I the only one who hasn't heard of this trail runner? But yeah. Gurpreet, you've done the file coordinator thing before right? I heard you did a good job of it. Would you like to do it again?"

"You bet, boss. That's my jam."

Davis's eyebrows pushed up his forehead, "Your jam? Okay. Sure. Brandon, Stacy, get caught up on the file, and then, get out to the house where this truck was seen. And then after that, I think we should interview Bibi and Matt. See what we can get from them."

Stacy: "Truck? And who?"

Davis: "Just read the file. Then you'll know."

Cameron: "What do you want me to do?"

Davis: "Start doing background workups on all the people mentioned in both cases. Social media presence, driver's license records, criminal records, if any, you know, everything you can find."

Cameron: "On it."

Stacy said to Brandon, "Let me know when you're finished reading the file and we'll get going."

"What if I finish reading it first?"

Stacy, turning her attention to her computer said, "Finish before me? Please."

-21-

Brandon finished reading the file. And twenty minutes after that, they were in their unmarked detective car and on their way to Mono Mills. Heading north from Hamilton, they traversed highways, four-lane roadways, and then single-lane roads where the danger lay in being stuck behind someone who drove the speed limit exactly or at an even slower rate. The cooler weather peeled the trees of their leaves. The grey sky painted the landscape in monotones, stealing the colour from the pastoral scenery.

Brandon was driving. He had quit smoking four months back and had substituted that oral fixation with the new one of chewing gum. The car smelled of Juicy Fruit and coffee. To Stacy, those smells were infinitely more preferable than cigarettes and coffee. She hoped Brandon would stay the course. He was a bit overweight, ate terribly, which was bad enough in this COVID climate, but if he'd kept smoking, his risk of a bad experience with COVID could be worse.

The police radio beeped a lone, high-pitched tone before going silent.

Stacy said, "We're out of range of the transmitter."

"Yeah."

A silent stretch continued as they passed barns in various states of disrepair.

Brandon said, "How much longer?"

"The phone says ten minutes."

"Can you hold it up so I can see it when we get closer?"

"Yup. I can do that."

"Wonder what this guy is all about."

She didn't answer. She knew what he meant. There wasn't anything in the file on the owner of the truck. Cameron, who was doing all the background work, didn't find much on their guy. There were no police reports in relation to the address, so Cameron had to request information from the Land Registry Office. The land, four acres of it, belonged to a Walt Griffin. Thirty-eight years old, zero social media presence, no tickets, no arrests, and strangely, no truck registered to him. He did have a Range Rover, a newer one, which implied money, only they didn't know what type of work he did. They had a driver's license photo of him. That's it. Stacy remembered Cameron showing it to them. White guy with a thick neck, wearing a hat, glasses, and a beard that would be the envy of any pre-industrial lumberjack.

Looking at the picture, Stacy asked Cameron, "Is this right? I thought they weren't allowed to wear a hat or glasses for those pictures."

"I know. Weird right?"

Stacy held up the phone for Brandon to see and said, "It says the place is three hundred metres up on the right."

"Gotcha. Number 4813, right?"

"That's right."

Brandon slowed down, signalled his intention, and turned off the paved road onto a gravel drive. Within ten feet, a metal gate barred their way. He stopped the car. Through the windshield, they could see a small bungalow with dark brown siding and a grey shingled roof about forty feet from the gate. Behind it, offset on the right, stood a garage of grey cinderblocks with a black garage door. Behind the garage, some distance away, a line of densely packed trees provided an impenetrable backdrop. The open field before the trees sprouted high, wild grass that poked out through the pockets of snow.

By the gate, an intercom hung from a metal post rising from the gravel.

Stacy said, "Okay. What do you wanna do?"

"Press the intercom?"

Brandon lowered the driver side window with a button. A gust of cold wind made him squint.

He depressed the button. From the speaker came the sound of a phone ringing.

A man's voice, "Hello?"

"Hello sir, I'm Detective Brandon Kleason with the Ontario Provincial Police. May we come in?"

"Who is we?"

"Is this Walt Griffin?"

"Who is the 'we' you mentioned? I'm assuming another officer?"

"Uh, yeah, Detective Stacy Strode is with me."

"What is your purpose for being here?"

"We're investigating a major case. And the investigation has led us here. A quick chat is all we need and then we'll be on our way."

"Major case? Like what? What does that mean?"

"Two abductions."

"Abductions? I'd like to help, but I'm sorry detectives. I don't feel comfortable letting anyone onto my property. With COVID and all, I don't meet with people I don't know."

"I understand. We've both been double vaccinated, and we have masks. How about if we meet outside? We could talk to you from your porch, or if you want, you could walk down here and talk to us from your side of the gate. Whatever makes you the most comfortable."

"I appreciate that. Only, my health isn't the best right now. I'd say I'm one of those high-risk people the news is always blathering on about, and because of that, I'm trying to stay away from everyone. And since no one is able to tell me if this can spread outside, so many contradictory opinions out there, I just don't feel safe taking any risks. I'm sure you understand."

Brandon gave Stacy a 'can you believe this?' look.

Stacy leaned over and said, "Look, we don't want to expose you to any unnecessary risks, but this is a very serious matter, and we need to talk to you."

"I just don't see how I can help. I've been stuck at home for months now."

"We're interested in your truck. That old blue one?"

"I don't have a truck like that. I have a Range Rover. Sorry I couldn't be of more help. I'm expecting a phone call from my doctor any minute now. I have to go. Take care detectives."

"Wait. Are you Walt Griffin?"

An audible click signalled the end of the conversation.

Brandon raised his window.

He said, "That went well, didn't it? All this driving for nothing."

"I wouldn't say that. See what he did? He didn't answer one question, except the one about the truck. He didn't even confirm his name and he did it under the pretense of being afraid of COVID."

"So what?"

"He said he was sorry he couldn't be of more help, but was he? More like he did everything he could to be the least helpful he could and under the guise of being COVID scared. I mean, the man didn't even confirm his name. We don't even know who we were speaking to. How do we know we were even talking to Walt Griffin? He has all the hallmarks, you know?"

"Hallmarks of what?"

"Of being a shifty motherfucker. One who now has my full and undivided attention."

-22-
EDUCATION PART 6

As expected, the killer was curious about his mother. Certain his father had killed her, he wondered why no one else had ever come looking for her. No family. No police. No one. How was that possible? Had his father killed everyone in her family? Of course not. That would be news for sure. So why?

On occasion, he would broach the subject of his mother to his father and depending on his father's mood, the killer would either receive violence or an expletive heavy sentence telling the killer that was not a subject up for discussion. He Googled his mother, but there wasn't a lot there. It seems she had followed his father's example and left little to no digital footprint.

Strange. He needed to know more about his mother, not for any nostalgic reason, but only to understand why her death meant nothing to anyone who might have known her. There was something there, something important to understand. It wasn't until years later that he understood he wanted to learn how to pick a victim and once he understood that he knew picking a victim left him more open to exposure. Randomness was the goal.

After his father had killed the conservation officer, he also learned the importance of location. Alone, in the woods, with no one around, death could be a mystery, an unsolved riddle. Even though the body had been somewhat clumsily hidden, as far as he knew, the conservation officer hadn't been found. He had learned from that incident without realizing that he had. He had stuffed it under the layers of information floating in his subconscious. He knew one day he would kill his father. His father knew it in the way a wild animal knew. His father could feel the danger lurking, ever-present, but unable to articulate or believe the source of the disquiet.

His father had secrets still. Identities, hidden money, and the ability to hide from the outside world while still contributing to it through taxes. The killer had much to learn from his father. But once class was over, he'd take out his knife, and get the answers he needed about the question that was his mother.

•   •   •

The killer stood a few feet back from his window, in the shadows, invisible from the road, watching the detectives in their car. They were discussing him out there. The truck. They had already traced the truck back to him. But how? The license plate wasn't shown in the image on the TV but that didn't mean the police didn't have the licence plate. It only meant they didn't share the information with the media. Even supposing they did have the plate, the truck wasn't registered to him or this address, so once again, how? Had a neighbour seen him in it? Possibly. But he only took the truck out at night. Like last night, when he had taken it out for the last time to dispose of it. Completely wiped clean, he had dumped the truck in a quarry lake and then hiked the eleven kilometres home. He did that to destroy the links in the chain tying him to any crime. No links, no jail. He hadn't expected they'd be at his door so soon. The detective car backed out of his driveway, paused, and headed back to wherever they had come from.

Did he do right? Taken by surprise, he questioned his actions. If he had let them in or allowed them to approach, they would have not only have seen him, they would potentially have controlled the interview. Keeping them away using COVID fear had the potential to deflect suspicion. He got the sense they hadn't bought what he had been endeavouring to sell but his reluctance to cooperate was a reasonable result of the paranoia affecting the nation and the world. Be wary of strangers. They may carry the plague. The end of the world doomsayers with their sandwich boards must be loving what was going on right now. They might feel vindicated in a way, pointing their accusatory fingers at their doubters while exclaiming, *I told you so!*

In the end, he was satisfied with how he had managed the situation. It was better for them to not have a description of him and to not pin him down to a story they could twist to their own ends at a later time.

Being cops, they'd be suspicious. They might send some people out to take a photo of him, follow him around, talk to his neighbours, the usual police prying bullshit. Good thing he didn't need to leave his home anytime soon.

-23-

Back at the office, Stacy said to Davis and the team, "Maybe we messed up. Maybe we should have kept the information about the truck as holdback evidence and set up on the man, Walt, or whoever he is."

Davis said, "Couldn't have been done. If we didn't show the truck, the neighbour never would have called us, and we never would have known where the guy lived. Also, Bibi wouldn't have seen the truck and we never would have known about the connection."

Stacy said, "Okay, I'll give you the neighbour, but the Major Case software would have picked up on the truck without Bibi."

"Maybe. Maybe not. Either way, we were better sharing the information than not."

"Yeah. I suppose, this once, you're right."

Brandon said, "So now what? Surveillance?"

Davis said, "I'll request it. We at least need to know who this guy is. But that's enough for today. You have Bibi and Matt coming in tomorrow for interviews?"

Stacy said, "Matt? First thing in the morning. Bibi said she'd be here before noon."

"All right. We'll reconvene at seven."

-24-

Max said, "There she is. The dog lady."

The four boys were sitting under a tree in the shade on the lawn of Taresh's home. Taresh was there with them, drinking from juice boxes his mom had provided for him and his friends. On an unusually hot day in October, the boys had been playing a game called Mankiller before their parents started calling them in for dinner. The previous snowfall from three days ago was all but gone with small pockets of it still surviving in the shade under trees. They all went to school together so the COVID restrictions on social interactions didn't apply to them since they were with each other all day, every day, in school. They did wear their masks most of the time. Except when eating or drinking. Like they were all doing now.

The dog lady had moved into their neighbourhood close to five years ago. It had been a big deal to Max's parents. She was famous or something but in a hushed-tone-sort-of-way. Not YouTube (LazarBeam was his favourite), Instagram or TikTok famous. She had done something; something real. Max had asked his parents what her deal was. They wouldn't tell him. Instead, they made him promise to leave her alone, and not to pester her with questions. They knew Max would go right up and ask her if they didn't tell him not to. His mom had her serious face on when she extracted his promise. The unblinking eyes and the little wrinkle at the corner of her mouth deepened, reinforcing the solemn nature of her request. Max promised not to bother the new neighbour, but he did what any ten-year-old would do when an adult was keeping a secret from them; he Googled her name. He knew her name because his parents had mentioned it, and what he found out, well, he just had to share it with his friends. She was like, a superhero, or as close as you could get without powers or being a revenge-seeking billionaire with parental abandonment issues.

Benny said, "Shush! She's coming this way."

Taresh said, "Why would we shush? That makes it weirder."

"I don't know. Then don't shush."

Sal said, "What do we talk about?"

Max said, "Guys, act normal. Drink your juice. We're just chilling."

Taresh said, "What's her name again?"

Max said, "Olivia."

"Right."

The sun hovered overhead travelling to the horizon, a bright orange rind of light, shining down on Olivia walking her dogs, not one of them on a leash, but all of them in Olivia's complete control. The dog in the lead pulled itself forward on a doggy wheelchair, mouth open, tongue out, a postcard-perfect image of a happy dog with the back portion of the animal secured to a red canvass chair on wheels. Olivia walked behind the red wheelchair. Two other dogs walked on either side of Olivia. All of them were German Shepherds. Olivia wore sunglasses, hair pulled back, and walked in complete control of her three bodyguards on four legs. The dogs walking to the side of her would occasionally glance up at Olivia as they walked, and seeing she was still there, would point their snouts forward again. The boys, forgetting to act natural, all stared at her as she approached, mouths open. The only sounds on the street were the approaching doggy chair wheels, the clip of nails on the sidewalk, and Olivia's soft steps.

As she got closer, Max looked for the details he'd read about. He saw two fingers missing from her right hand and a tingle started in his belly. With her hair pulled back, he saw a nub and a hole where her ear used to be. The arm of her sunglasses was tucked into the tight line of her hair. The hairs on his arm stood. What he had read about her was true. It was all true.

"Boys."

Max blinked. She had nodded to them, talked to them and continued on her way. When she was out of hearing range, Taresh said, "Did you see her ear?"

Benny said, "No, I was looking at her hand."

Sal said, "I know right? Gross."

Max frowned. Gross? How were they gross? They were battle scars. Earned with her blood. Even then, those physical marks didn't diminish her in any way in Max's eyes. He didn't know what it was, how to describe what it was that Olivia possessed. If he was older, he might have said she had presence. Her aura made you feel real, made you feel tangible instead of floating thoughts residing behind a pair of eyes, watching the world, but not a participant in it. But he didn't know that word, he only knew how she made him feel. Instead, he used a word he understood. Max said, "Nah. She's fucking cool."

The other boys laughed at him.

Taresh said, "Max is in love!"

Benny said in a high falsetto, "Oh Olivia, you're so fucking cool, I love you!"

Max smiled, drank the rest of his juicebox, stood, handed the empty box to Taresh and said, "I'll catch you guys later."

They laughed some more.

Sal said, "Max is mad! Poor baby!"

Max wasn't mad. After seeing Olivia, playing Mankiller seemed like kid-stuff. And he wasn't in the mood for it anymore. Not for today at least. He had more Googling to do. He thought maybe his wall needed another picture beside his Superman poster. One of Olivia would do. Yeah, that'd be about perfect.

•   •   •

Olivia finished her walk, brought the dogs inside, and turned on the kettle. She still wasn't used to the stares, and if it wasn't for her dogs, she wouldn't venture out in public as often as she did. She had moved from the home where Harry had been killed. The memories were hard there. Like they had been plucked from her mind and carved of stone, unyielding, forever reminding statues commemorating her failure to protect the man who had done so much for her. She moved to escape the memories, and the media looked for their soundbites with their cameras and microphones, the rough pry bar tools of their profession in order to showcase her pain and her terror for the public's entertainment. To her, it seemed the media was less about news and more about clickbait titles sensationalizing everything. Even if the topic didn't deserve it. And her moving to escape had worked to a degree. She moved to a suburb in London, Ontario, but apparently, that wasn't far enough. Her neighbours knew who she was, and because of that, so did the local children. She couldn't hide her mangled hands or ears, especially in the summer. And soon enough, people nodded at her, not sure if they should smile at her or not and their expressions would fluctuate from stern to friendly to anxious. Olivia nodded back and did nothing to help them welcome her into their neighbourhood. She didn't want any new friends. They'd ask questions. They'd pry. And she didn't have the patience or the emotional strength for that. Better to be alone and focus on her one friend: Davis. And, to a lesser extent, her uncle Frank, more of a stranger than he ever had been. The cards sent on her birthday and Christmas had been the extent of his contact after Harry's funeral. If that's what he wanted to be to her, a twice-a-year-card-relative, then that's what he would be.

The boiling water brought her out of her reverie. She dropped a bag into her cup, poured water on it and while it steeped, she lifted Brutus out of his doggie wheelchair (remembering to use her legs and not her back), and placed him on his dog bed. Her other two dogs, Freya and Odin, sat before their empty water bowls waiting for her.

It had warmed up outside considerably over the last two days and she didn't need to wear her spring coat during her walk, but she did because it allowed her to carry her knife on her hip, hidden by the drape of the coat. You really never knew who was out there watching, waiting for you to let your guard down even for an instant because an instant was all it took. She had learned that lesson. She had learned it in the hardest way imaginable. Her eyes were drawn to the picture of Harry on the counter by the stove. She blinked.

She fed and watered her dogs and sat down with her tea drifting steam. Down the hall, she saw that she locked the front door. She knew she had, she never failed to do so before, but sometimes when an action becomes a habit, the remembering of it doesn't occur, as though the mind fails to record what it deems unworthy.

"Alexa: play *This is Taylor Swift* on Spotify."

Playing This is Taylor Swift on Spotify.

Lover began and Olivia's shoulders dropped. She needed the background noise. Anything to stop her brain from inserting images of a pink cell behind her eyes, the snip of Craftsman pruning shears, the sweaty smell of men pinning her down. Davis suggested therapy to her once. And she thought that maybe for some people, most people even, that was a good idea. She couldn't stomach the thought. She'd have to sit in a room, with some stranger, on a dark leather sofa because that's what was always in one of those rooms, and she'd have to talk and tell this person what it was like to be living in a body that didn't belong to you. It belonged to two men in masks who had taken her off the street, from a place that was supposed to be safe and did things to Olivia that shamed her even to recall them. Intellectually she knew none of it had been her fault. That the shame and the blame lay with the two dead psychos she had killed. Knowing that and feeling that were two different concepts. Rationalization did not make the boogeyman less real to a child who was afraid of what lurked in the closet after the lights went out. And it did her no service to lay the blame where it was deserved no matter how rational, how logical that conclusion was. Her guilt was a vile poison, diminishing her with every negative thought, and therapy seemed counter-intuitive to her. How could she expect to get over something by talking about it, reliving it, over and over again? Examining the minutiae of every degradation she was forced to submit to and then failing the only person who loved her unconditionally... how could that possibly help her? You don't pick at a scab to speed the healing process. You don't pull the stitches out of your skin before it has healed. She sipped at her tea. Her cell phone rang in her pocket, startling her. She brushed away a tear that escaped her eye and trailed down her cheek.

"Hello?"

"You in the mood for dinner and company tonight?"

"Davis! How are you? And yes."

"I'm good. You okay?"

Had he heard the sadness in her voice? Was he that in tune with her?

"Yeah. I'm good. Surrounded by my furry kids, why wouldn't I be?"

"Your pack looking after you? Good. What do you want to do for dinner, then?"

"Well, with COVID, we don't have many options, do we? I'm feeling Five Guys... you good with that?"

"You bet. I'll pick it up and see you in a couple of hours, cool?"

"Yeah. Oh, and bring Sandra would ya? Haven't seen her in a while."

"That was the plan. Text me what you want."

"Will do. See you soon."

-25-

When Rori arrived home from work, she found Bibi on the couch, chin resting on her knees with her arms wrapped around her shins. She was staring at the TV, which wasn't on. She didn't notice Rori walk into the room.

"Good show?"

Bibi blinked, as though awakening from a dream, frowned at Rori, and Rori thought, *she doesn't know me*, and her stomach clenched as though bracing for a punch.

"Rori. Hey."

"What's going on? Are you ok?"

"I don't know. Seeing that truck brought it all back. I can smell the pine trees, the dirt, my own sweat. I can see him, the silhouette of him, a murderous shadow. I can hear his voice. All of it, like it happened this morning, running through my head like a song on repeat. I thought I got over it, not entirely, but enough to function."

"That's normal. And you will get over it, eventually. It'll just take more time."

"I didn't go to work today. I didn't call and tell them either. I didn't even think of calling them. Like I forgot I had a job. I couldn't think, can't think, of anything else except for how close to death I was. And seeing that truck, you know what else I can't stop thinking about?"

"What?"

"How many other people has he done this to? How many didn't escape like me? And what did he do to them before they died?"

A tear spilled from her eye.

Rori said, "The police know now. They know he exists."

Bibi, through gritted teeth, said, "They already knew. I told them! And they slept on it! For five years!"

Rori said, "Maybe they did. But they're awake now. Because of you, they're awake."

"They want me to go to their station, near Hamilton, for an interview tomorrow."

"You going to go?"

"Of course. I'm so angry at them, though. The only good thing is the detective I'm supposed to talk to tomorrow. He worked on the Jackal case."

"What case?"

"The big murder-rape thing from like five years ago? Where the creeps kept women prisoner?"

"Ok. Yeah. Wasn't there another animal in that case?"

"Yeah. A Gorilla. Anyway, he worked that. He might understand. He might be able to find my guy. I don't know what I'm going to say. I don't think I'll be able to stop myself from giving them crap for sitting on this for so long. Now, with that poor man taken, to say 'I told you so' seems petty and childish. I don't think they are going to like me all that much."

Rori said, "So what? What does that even matter?"

Bibi shivered and said, "I don't know. I can't think. I see him all the time, you know? Can't eject the fuck from my brain. I'm sorry. I feel so useless. I'm supposed to be tough, and here I am, living with you guys. I feel like such an intruder."

"Intruder?" Rori sat beside Bibi and put her arms around her and rested her head on Bibi's shoulder.

Rori said, "Bibi. You're family. You know that, right? You're no intruder."

Bibi said, "I hate him. I would kill him if I could. To have this power over me… I can't stand it."

"I know. You might want to give therapy another try. Who knows? You might find someone who can help. And with COVID, you can do the therapy at home, on ZOOM, from your computer."

"I don't know. Maybe."

Bibi didn't want to tell her friend she had given up on therapy. Sitting in a room, in front of a person with a notepad and pen, asking her how she felt about this or that, and that person, living their safe sterile life, trying to help her get over that day that was impossible to get over. Not with that man still out there. What did they know of fear? What did they know of terror? How could they possibly help her with something they had never experienced? Like trying to describe the colour blue to a blind person. There was no base reference of communication and although they spoke the same language, the meanings, the connection between the words were miles apart. Give her someone to talk to that knew what it meant to wait out a day, tied up, knowing that at the conclusion of that day, after the sun went down, you'd be dead. Give her someone who understood captivity.

-26-

Behind Olivia, to greet Davis and Sandra sat Freya and Odin. Their tales swished the floor free of dust, but they didn't whine. They wouldn't even think of it. They were well trained. Brutus leaned forward off his mat to see them as well and if he could have wagged his tail, it most definitely would be cleaning the floor too.

Davis held the bag of food and Sandra held the tray of drinks. They both wore soft blue masks, the kind seen in hospitals. The smell of the burgers and the fries raised a smile on Olivia's face. She said, "The food's here. And Sandra! Thank gawd for that! Haven't seen you in ages!" She said 'god' like an easterner, 'gawd', not because she was from out east, but because she liked the way it sounded.

Davis frowned, "What about me? You didn't mention me."

"Didn't I? Are you sure? I'm pretty sure that I *always* mention who's important to me. Come in, you two. I'm starving. My stomach must think my throat has been cut."

Davis stepped inside, wrinkling his nose, and said, "What's going on? Have you been watching some Newfie shows? Or reading some books from out east?"

"Nah. Just some memes I've seen."

"Ah. Memes. I'm done talking to you. I'll eat with you, though."

●　　●　　●

Sandra and Davis, after putting the bags and tray on the kitchen table, paid their respects to Freya, Odin, and Brutus. Seated, with the food allocated to the proper persons, they ate, talked, got sidetracked on COVID politics, and once finished with their meal, Olivia started brewing a pot of coffee.

Olivia said, "What do you take in your coffee, Sandra?"

"A splash of milk, is all."

Davis said, "What about me?"

"I know what you take, Davis. Relax. How do you deal with him? Always wanting attention?"

Sandra said, "It's a burden."

Olivia delivered the coffee, sat down, and she smiled, "Doesn't coffee smell the best?"

Davis said, "Agreed," and he sipped on his.

A lull in the conversation, but not an uncomfortable one. These were people who liked each other, and their silences didn't need to be filled. Sometimes, silences are comforting with friends.

"Anything exciting going on at work? Any unlawful arrests, illegal searches, you know, police work?"

"Hilarious. And no."

"Owen, tell Olivia about that new case you've been assigned."

Olivia said, "Owen," Olivia laughed, "I forget you have a first name sometimes."

"Me too. Sandra's the only person who calls me that. Well, except for my parents."

Olivia said, "Go on. Do tell about this new, exciting case."

"I don't know if it's exciting yet. Interesting… yes. But I guess there is excitement potential."

Sandra said, "Spit it out already."

And he did.

•　　•　　•

Davis started with Bibi. And the more he spoke, the more motionless Olivia became. She had been twirling her coffee cup by the rim with the tips' of her fingers and her thumb, but then she stopped, her eyes unblinking, focused on Davis. The capture, the threat, the harrowing night in a hole, and her fortunate escape. Throughout the tale, Olivia's colour shifted through all the shades. She swallowed once before Davis started on the tale of Ken, and before he got to the end, Olivia's forehead sported orbs of sweat, and her breath shortened.

Davis, frowning, said, "Are you ok? Listen, I'm going to stop now, all right? Do you want a glass of cold water or something? You don't look so hot."

Olivia blinked. A line of sweat crested her right eyebrow.

"I'm fine. Really. I, uh, I'm really tired. I think I'm going to call it an early night."

Sandra stood and leaned forward with an arm outstretched to touch Olivia's shoulder. Before her fingers could brush her, Olivia pushed back from the table and stood. One hand went to her waist, where her knife was in its sheath on her belt. Freya, Odin and Brutus growled.

Olivia said, "Quiet!"

The dogs quieted.

Olivia's hands dropped to her sides. She stared at the table but spoke to Davis and Sandra. She said, "I'm sorry. The tying up, the attack, it uh, brought things back to me, harder than I thought they could be brought back. I thought I was almost over this, this helplessness. It's a little too much. I need some time. To myself. I'm sorry. I feel like such a loser sometimes."

Davis said, "Don't apologize to me, Olivia. I'm the idiot who told you all that. I should have known better."

Sandra said, "Nope. My fault. I told you to tell her. Owen and I are the only losers here. Well, Owen for sure. But me? I'm the mayor of Losertown."

Still looking at the table, Olivia said, "Ok. I love you guys. But get out of here."

•　　•　　•

The first fifteen minutes into the drive home, Davis and Sandra didn't speak. *Plush* by Stone Temple Pilots played on the radio. Davis cracked open the driver side window as their burger breath was getting to be too much.

Sandra broke the silence first: "I really messed up."

"No."

"I should have thought of that, but I didn't. You talked cases with her before, so maybe I thought that's why this time would be fine, but not like that. Not a case so similar to what had happened to her."

"You couldn't have known she'd react as she did. I didn't know, and I know her the best out of the both of us. I only feel bad because she feels bad. She's been through enough. More than enough."

"She needs someone to talk to."

"She's tried. Plenty of times. I asked around at work, talked to one of the shrinks that are on retainer to talk to us cops, you know, shrinks who know about trauma, and she didn't take to any of them."

"You know, no one calls them shrinks anymore."

"I do. I'm somebody, aren't I?"

Sandra rolled her eyes and smiled at the same time.

Davis said, "I don't know. I think she needs to talk to someone to who she can relate. Someone who, when they say they understand her, they actually do and it's not just that thing shrinks say."

"Yeah. Maybe. I wish I could help her. She's breaking my heart."

"Mine too."

-27-

Davis interviewed Bibi. The original statement she had given five years ago was good. The investigator asked relevant questions and Bibi provided detailed answers. Really, the only purpose of this secondary interview, years later, was to document the truck she had seen on TV and why she believed it was the same truck she had seen on the day of her abduction. Bibi struck him as smart and tough. Scarred though. Like scratch marks on a gold bar.

When the interview was over and the camera turned off, Bibi asked, "Did you… were you the one who worked on the Jackal case? That was you right?"

They were standing in a typical police hallway outside of the interview room. Fluorescent overhead lighting, cinderblock walls painted a soft grey, people walking past staring at a phone in their hand or a piece of paper, looking very busy and important, or pretending to be to avoid the dreaded, "Are you busy?" question that preceded a lost weekend at work. Bibi's eyes shifted from side to side, stopping on people in the hallway and then returning to Davis.

Davis said, "Yeah. I did."

"There was something in the news after, something about you and the woman, Olivia? I got the feeling you guys were pretty close."

Davis stiffened. This wasn't the first time someone insinuated the feelings he had for Olivia went beyond the professional.

"Look-"

"Are you still friends?"

Bibi rubbed her hands together and peered at him with something like hope. Davis realized she wasn't accusing; she was asking for a personal reason and the reason had weight to it.

"Yeah. We're good friends."

"Ok. I know you don't have to tell me. She's your friend. I get it. But is she ok? Like with all that happened? Has she moved on?"

Davis understood right then that Bibi was struggling. And he remembered Olivia from last night, and that she was still struggling. Bibi wanted to know for comparison with herself. If Olivia was still messed up, after all that happened to her, then it would be ok for her to be messed up too, right? Then she'd be normal, whatever that means. What could he say though? Olivia was his friend and to tell this stranger her problems, that's just not what friends did. Bibi gazed at him, eyes shiny, looking for validation from someone who couldn't give it. That had to come from within and the person had to find it for themselves.

"That's complicated. I think that's a question only she could answer."

Bibi glanced down, her rounded shoulders describing her defeat.

"Would you like me to ask her to call you?"

Bibi rubbed her arms, hugging herself and said, "She wouldn't be, like, annoyed?"

"Of course not."

"Then yeah, please. That'd be… that'd be pretty terrific."

-28-

"What the hell, Davis?"

Turned out, Olivia was annoyed, bordering on angry.

Davis, in his office, with Bibi's and Ken's case file opened and on the two computer screens before him, thought he'd give Olivia a call and ask her if she'd like to talk to Bibi. He had expected a little reluctance on her part, but not this almost-anger riding the timbre of her voice.

"What? I only told her I'd ask you to call her. I didn't say you would."

"Oh yeah? And what does that make me look like if I don't call her? A bitch! That's what! I can't believe you sometimes."

"I didn't think of that at all."

"Clearly! When you volunteered your hermit-doesn't-like-other-people-friend to call a complete stranger?"

"I was thinking, fuck, I don't know. Wait, I do know, kind of... I was thinking that you have no one to talk to about your experiences, right? Who can relate to what you've endured, lived through, and have to deal with every day? Bibi was there, in front of me, and all but begging me to tell her that one day, she'll get over what happened to her. That one day, she'll wake up and not be frightened anymore, and I couldn't tell her that. Because my great friend is still struggling and maybe, just maybe, my friend needs someone to talk to as well. A someone who has an inkling, a smidgen of an idea of what you experienced, and even if you can't get through it together, you could be a support system for each other that is based on both of your terrible experiences. I love you, Olivia. It hurts me to know you're hurting, and I thought, maybe, you and Bibi could help each other."

Breathing on both ends.

Davis heard an argument from the open door of his office. Through the glass, he saw Cam pointing a finger at Stacy. Cam was red-faced. Stacy wore a smirk. Oh-oh.

Olivia said, "You thought all that did you?"

"Not in the moment, no. It occurred to me later?"

"Is that a question?"

Outside in the office, *"The fucking government telling us to wear a mask everywhere is bullshit!"*

Olivia said, "What's going on? Is that, is that in your office?"

"I gotta go."

Davis ended the call and left his office thinking; *I wish I had failed that stupid promotional exam!*

•   •   •

Davis extinguished the political office fire and asked Stacy, in private, not to provoke Cam into his rage mode over COVID or any other government policy he disagreed with. After that was done, he read the transcript of the interview with Matt, Ken's partner. Poor guy. If anyone wanted to know what a broken heart read like, they should read Matt's interview. Devastated didn't begin to describe the impact Ken's abduction had on him.

His phone beeped. He looked at it, saw it was a text from Olivia. It read: *Send me her number. I might call her… one of these days, and only if I feel like it.*

Davis smiled and texted Bibi's phone number to Olivia.

-29-

In almost all major case investigations, there'd be a daily meeting to discuss updates and prioritize tasks and assign them accordingly. There had been two major interviews today with Matt and Bibi, and a minor one with the neighbour who had seen the truck in her neighbour's garage. Davis thought it would be good to review the interviews to see if any new tasks were generated as a result of the interviews to help strategize for the next day.

Stacy asked, "Anything back from the Inspector on the surveillance?"

Davis said, "Yeah. The Inspector is all for it. The Intel guys, however, were less than impressed."

Brandon said, "What's their problem?"

Davis said, "Normally, we have more for them to work with. For this guy, we have a shitty driver's license photo and that's it. We haven't found any background on the guy and he's left no mark on the social media world so, that's their first problem."

Brandon: "They have more than one?"

"Yeah. Where this guy lives, there's no place to set up that doesn't scream *'Cops here!'* He lives in a rural area with no nearby buildings or parking lots to hide a cop in a car. Anything new in the area would be noticed immediately."

Cam said, "So their job is hard this time. Boo-hoo."

Stacy said, "But they're going to do it, right? The surveillance? That guy, even if he's not involved in this, he's involved in something. Got my spidey senses all tingling."

-30-
EDUCATION PART 7

Flaying a person had been harder than he thought it would be. It was an error to think it would be easy, but he did, and the frustration of the whole enterprise made him vow to never do it again.

The initial set-up had been easy and maybe that fuelled his confidence for the rest. His father, after being awake for five days fuelled by paranoia, coffee and generous portions of speed, finally crashed from exhaustion. He fell asleep at the table while talking about drones following him around in the field whenever he left the house. Continuously talking, specks of foam in the corners of his mouth, yammering, "They're getting closer, the government have eyes everywhere, watching, waiting to take away everything I earned. They don't like people who are too free, you see? People who don't buy all the happy-horseshit they shovel out to the masses, they hate those people. People like me. They don't want it to spread, you see, they don't want other people seeing the freedom I have and then wanting it for themselves, the sons a' bitches. I'm on to them. Their drones, the listening in on our phones. Did you know they could turn on the mics on our phones? They don't need to sneak in and install bugs like in the old days. No. We bring in the bugs for them! We do their dirty work! Can you believe that? Tracking our internet too. That's why I got that IP hider. The sons a' bitches! Always want more don't they?"

He stared at the tabletop, swaying, blinking his eyes and shaking his head to stay awake. He collapsed to the floor. A tank crashing into their home wouldn't have woken him up.

The killer picked him up and carried him outside to the shed where they prepped and skinned the animals they killed. His father, who didn't weigh much more than a wet fart, had him struggling to move him only twenty feet. He decided to work on that. In order to pursue his passion, he'd need to improve his cardio and strength. The simple fact became more apparent after he bound his father by wrist and ankle to the rack used for animal prepping. He had to hold him standing upright to secure his father's wrists above head. If he had developed his strength, the feat would have been easier.

Once he had secured his father, the killer sharpened a straight razor. He liked the look of it and the feel of it in his hand. Once sharpened, he cut off his father's filthy shirt and then left him there. He returned to their home, cleaned the kitchen, opened the windows to rid the place of his father's stink, and made himself a sandwich. He ate the sandwich, drank a soda, and glanced at the calendar on the wall. The calendar was from two years ago and opened to the month of his birthday. He'd be twenty in eight days. He'd be free of his father in about twelve hours. Depending on how long his father would last, of course.

He removed a bucket from under the sink. He filled it with cold water. He walked out to the shed, his feet squishing through the crushed gravel. He opened the shed door. His father, standing upright in the awkward-tied-to-a-rack position, slept with his chin on his chest. Drool, shiny and thick, hung from his lip and swayed like a pendulum in line with his belly button.

He tossed the cold water from the bucket at his father's face.

His father jerked awake, spun his head from side to side, stared up to his bound wrists and down to his bound ankles. The crazy eyes found the killer's face next.

"Who put you up to this? The Prime Minister? The RCMP? Who?"

"I put myself up to this. I have questions for you. I'm inclined to make you answer them."

His father smiled. The brown teeth almost blended in with the dark beard. His eyes burned like bonfires trapped in his skull.

"You'll never make me talk. And you'll never get my money." He giggled.

"I already have the money. That wasn't hard to take from you. In your more lucid moments, you might even remember that you showed me how."

His father pulled at the restraints.

"Who do you work for? Are you even my son?"

The killer picked up the razor. He said, "I need you to focus. Okay? None of this government crap. I work for me. I want to know more about my mother. And you're going to tell me about her."

"I ain't got nothing to say about the whore."

"Maybe not now. But you will."

The killer, with complete focus, flayed the skin from his father's right forearm. The problem with flaying was that blood makes everything slippery. It made his razor handle slippery, and the skin itself, covered in blood, became hard to grip and peel from the muscle. And with his father screaming in his ear, a headache started to bloom behind his eyes.

•   •   •

He had peeled the skin off both arms and the right side of his father's chest before his father told him all he wanted to know.

His father had picked up his mother on the side of the road, outside of a truck stop. She had been a prostitute and her last customer, a truck driver, after completion of the deed, refused to drive her back to where he had picked her up from. The truck driver had a delivery to make in the morning, and he needed his sleep.

At the time of their courtship, his father wasn't completely batshit crazy although there were signs that he was on his way. His mother didn't pick up on those flashes of crazy until it had been too late. She had fled her home after being dumped on her grandparents' doorstep because her own mother had died of a drug overdose. She had been exposed to the lifestyle of an addict and learned early on that until her mother kicked her habit, she would always be last on her daily to-do list which consisted of only one item: getting high. His mother, a person born to be a victim, had been taken in by his father, because in her short life, here was a man who had convinced her that she was important and that her happiness was also important to him and how could she not fall for that given the environment she'd been moulded by? And fall she did. He took her to his home, told her she wouldn't have to work, told her he'd take care of her, and with an eloquence he once possessed, turned his life-hardened mother into a person with hope. She saw a future with him and a family she had never had but could have. And this person, with no one to care for her or look for her, was perfect for someone like his father. Because if she disappeared, who would care to look? She had no one. And to his father, she was no one.

The killer learned from his father an aspect of victimology he would use to his later benefit. If a person went missing in a way the police or family didn't find suspicious, the resources to find the person would be spent in full at the beginning. After some time had passed, the police would go away. The family might forever hope, but in their hearts, they'd know that more often than not, hope was a fool's dream. Location and victim circumstances were crucially important in the pursuit of killing while remaining invisible. He didn't think of it in that manner at the time. It was something that percolated and brewed and had a hand (an invisible one) in the development of his rules for murder.

With all of his questions answered, he cut his father's throat with the razor.

He buried him beside his mother.

He renovated the home and then sold the property. He moved to his present home and ruminated on life and the exquisite beauty in ending that most fragile gift.

•　　•　　•

The killer sat cross-legged on a yoga mat, meditating on how to proceed. He had just finished a heavy lifting session, followed by his hundred's workout for cardio. One hundred burpees, one hundred squats, one hundred push-ups and fifty pull-ups. Fifty for the last exercise because pull-ups are harder than the other exercises. The circuit was done for time, and you couldn't move on to the next exercise until you completed the hundred reps needed. He pushed himself hard. Almost to the point of nausea. He wasn't satisfied with a workout unless his vision grew dark on the edges and spots of light crowded his sight. After such a session, he'd stretch and practice breathing exercises while meditating. His workout sessions were scheduled for every other day, but he meditated every day. He always felt great afterward. A strong current of electricity firing the neurons and synapses in his brain, made him feel more alert, more alive, long after he finished the meditation.

Today was different though. The cops were sniffing around, and he was considering what to do about it. They didn't know who he was, so that was good, but they knew where he lived, which wasn't good. Now, what should he do about it? Could he stop killing indefinitely?

He thought a good habit to employ in the interest of self-betterment was to learn how to be overly critical of oneself. Peel back the layers with no shame, no judgement, only an honest evaluation of strengths and weaknesses. Had he come to rely on killing as a means of intense... what's the word? Entertainment? Could he find something else to do? He thought it through knowing the importance of the answer. There was no evidence of his crimes. No person and no equipment used in the killing of those persons could be traced back to him. No DNA would be found, and unless they found him standing over a corpse with the murder weapon in his hand, right now, he was home free. They hadn't even found the remains of a victim yet.

Without a victim, there could be no nexus of evidence drawn to him and even with a victim, because of the selected randomness, they couldn't tie any one of them to him. The killer was aware of the laws, had studied them, and he knew the police would need a judge who couldn't read or understand the law to be willing to sign a warrant for them to search his home. No such judge existed as far as he knew. So, he was safe. But could he be safer? If he stopped killing, he'd be completely safe. Without any more crimes, there was nothing to investigate, and he'd fade into the police background. He'd be bored out of his mind, but safe. Could he live like that? Sure. He felt confident that he could stop. The real question was, did he need to? Could he even turn the police involvement into an advantage? Use the police to clear him?

His habitat of isolation afforded him an unfordable moat against surveillance. If the police were out there, he'd see them. There was nowhere they could hide from him. A panorama of flat farmland with no buildings, their presence would be conspicuous in and of itself. If they did start watching him, and if he could make them believe he was home when he was actually out taking his next victim, they'd provide him with an alibi. They'd never be able to pin a murder on him after that. A dangerous but excellent plan. Dangerous, because right now, in his home, he was safe. If he ventured out and they stopped him, he'd be forced to identify himself. The public had no idea of the many ways that existed for the police to detain, even arrest someone, if they didn't identify themselves. But he did.

He had good IDs, but he didn't want to expose any of them to official scrutiny. They might not hold up and that would create a whole new list of problems. His home was registered to Walt Griffin, and so was the Range Rover, and for now, he was happy that was all the police had to work with. If they caught him outside, they might dig deeper than he'd want them to. Not that there was anything there to find. He operated under three main identities for different purposes. Not one of them was the name he had been given at birth. He hadn't been born in a hospital. Thanks to his father's paranoia, there was no record of his birth. He had to create one, just so he could own a home and pay taxes. From birth, he was a person with no name. He liked that. Poetic even. The reason for such security precautions wasn't for poetic reasons. He knew, from a young age, that he wanted to kill people. A vocation such as that demanded that he become an invisible man. An untraceable one. He had been traced to his home, which, annoyed him considerably. He didn't know how the police had done it. That truck hadn't been registered to him or this address so how they ended up at the bottom of his driveway asking questions about the truck on the news was baffling. Not knowing the 'how' made him nervous. If he couldn't figure out how they ended up at his home, how could he take steps to prevent further incursions? He had to get them looking somewhere else. If they decided to spy on him, he might be able to turn that to his advantage. Like pulling off an abduction while the police were watching him. That'd be epic.

He contemplated. He breathed in, breathed out and felt his mind expand. His body melted away. His mind emptied. A blackboard wiped clean. In that state of nothingness, he waited for an answer to make itself known.

-31-

Olivia, surrounded by her dogs, held a cup of coffee in her hand, while sitting in front of the TV. *Sex Education* played on the screen. The type of witty show that could normally hold her attention failed to do so this evening. Her brain spun within her skull, and that's how she pictured it, loose in there, grey wrinkly matter spinning and spinning. She couldn't make it stop. Sometimes she could force her mind to be calm, to be present, and experience the moment, even if the moment lacked any value. Despite her best efforts, her brain wouldn't quit. She knew why, too. The number Davis had sent her through text ran through her mind, as though it had been stamped on it. She wanted to call Bibi and she didn't want to call Bibi at the same time. A tug of war in constant motion within her brain, with the burning phone number blazing in the middle, being pulled back and forth with equal force. One side pulling was labelled 'hope' and the other side was labelled 'fear'.

She inhaled the scent of the coffee, sipped it, and reached down to pat Brutus on the head. He groaned with pleasure.

What was she hoping for? Someone who knew her, without actually knowing her. A shared experience of terror that bound them to each other at the soul. Bibi, although her horror experience lasted two days, Bibi knew what it meant to be helpless, to fear, and to believe with all her heart that the end of her capture will result in her death. A horrible, painful, and humiliating death. Lucy had known Olivia's fear, and she hoped they could be friends, except Lucy wanted to forget it all. For her memory to be wiped clean, Lucy needed to get rid of everyone who reminded her of the events. Lucy failed to realize for that to happen, she would need to get rid of herself. Or maybe she did know that because the last Olivia had heard, Lucy started using drugs to dull the pain. From there, the downhill slide found Lucy homeless. Olivia sometimes wondered where Lucy was and if she knew, what would she do about it? Would she try to rescue her, like she tried to with her father and his alcoholism? Maybe.

She could have a friend like that. Someone who knew and didn't pretend to know while nodding their head and offering stupid platitudes like *time heals all wounds*. What a stupid thing to say. Not all wounds heal. Olivia's ear, toes and fingers attested to that. And she knew that's not what they meant. They meant wounds of the heart. And that may be true, but to hear the bullshit spoken by someone who doesn't know what fear is, what violence is, what degradation truly means, was, to put it bluntly, fucking infuriating. Someone, other than Lucy, who knew and understood the illusion of safety was just that, an illusion. But it might lessen her feeling of being alone. People talk of safety like it was something real, something tangible. Only Olivia, Lucy, and maybe Bibi knew that safety was no more substantial than smoke. Bibi might know, and that would be… good. She was given the phone number for Bibi. All she had to do was call. Fear stalled her intent.

It welled up from the pit of her stomach and trembled the cup in her hand. Bibi might not know. May not even understand, even a little bit, of what Olivia had gone through. That was possible. And then Olivia would be right back here, where she started, with no one to talk to, no one to help lighten the never-ending weight on her shoulders. And then there was Harry. Would she be able to disclose to Bibi how she had failed the one person on this planet who never gave up on her? Who always held hope close to his heart, holding it to his chest as though he were protecting a candle flame from the wind? Would she be able to withstand the look of disgust on Bibi's face if she ever disclosed the truth of her failure? Goddamnit. Would she ever stop feeling afraid? How many more dogs would she need to feel safe? She blew a breath she didn't realize she'd been holding out through her nose. The real question, the one she should have asked herself hours ago was, what would Harry want me to do?

She knew the answer. Which was why she avoided asking it.

She dialled the number.

"Hello?"

"Bibi?"

"Yes."

"This is Olivia Barnes."

Olivia heard an inhale of breath.

"Oh, you called, I mean you're calling. Thank you. You don't know how much this mean to-"

Olivia heard Bibi sobbing on the other end. Odd, but to hear Bibi cry made Olivia glad she had called. Still nervous, but glad all the same. There it was again, the flickering flame of hope. And there was no Harry here to protect it.

-32-

"There is no place to watch this guy from."

Using a projector and Google Maps, a map of Walt Griffin's home filled the four-foot by six-foot whiteboard screen. The six-person team from Intelligence, the surveillance unit, stood at the back of the room. Davis and Stacy drove down to the office of the Intelligence unit for a strategy meeting. The office, hidden in an out-of-the-way industrial complex, was hard to find if you hadn't been there before. They wanted to keep their location a secret for obvious reasons and most officers within the OPP didn't know where the Intelligence unit was located. You had to be invited as Davis had been.

Davis, standing beside the supervisor from Intelligence, Benny, rubbed his chin while studying the map. Benny wasn't kidding. There really was nothing out there. The small house stood behind a steel gate at the end of the driveway. A wire fence running along the southern border of the property disappeared into the treeline on the north end of the property, and that was that. No buildings nearby, no homes, not even a water tower to break the flat horizon.

Stacy said, "Is he growing anything out there?"

Davis said, "According to the neighbour, who told us the truck was there, no, he is not."

Benny said, "Do we know how he makes his money? Where he goes grocery shopping? Banking? Anything?"

Stacy said, "The house is registered to Walt Griffin, thirty-eight years of age, white male, and that's pretty much it. We don't know where he works, how he pays for anything, or even if he has a Costco membership. We don't even know if the guy who talked to us through the speaker was Walt Griffin. For all we know, Walt Griffin could be renting the place out and the guy we spoke to was the tenant."

Benny tilted his head to the side and frowned at Davis. He said, "Davis. We're going to need more. What are we looking at here? A guy who might have owned a truck seen at the scene of an abduction? That's it?"

Davis said, "Two abductions."

Benny: "Five years apart? I read the file. Five years is a long time. How could she be sure it's the same-"

Davis said, "She's sure. I interviewed her. She's sure. And I believe her."

"All right. What were you hoping we could do for you?"

"Find out who the hell is living in that house. That'd be a great start. Who's paying the taxes? Can't we find that out?"

Stacy said, "Warrant."

Benny turned his attention back to the map and said, "Speaking of warrants, without one, we can't even go onto the property. Not one toe over the fence line."

Davis said, "I know."

"You getting a warrant?"

"With what we have? No one would sign it."

A pause. All heads were turned to the screen.

Benny said, "Davis, my friend, you're, how do I say this delicately? You're kind of fucked here."

Davis sighed and said, "Yeah. I know. But we gotta do something."

They continued to follow all of their investigative leads to their conclusion and what they concluded was they didn't have much to work with. The investigation stalled for four months, two weeks and five days. Because on the following day, Ken's body was discovered.

-33-

The place where the killer buried Ken sat near a nickel mine. When creating new tunnels in the mine for the miners to work in, explosives were used. The preferred explosive used was ANFO (Ammonium Nitrate Fuel Oil) because the charges could be directed and, more or less, controlled. The explosion that unearthed Ken had been detonated almost a kilometre away and at least two kilometres underground. The charge had been set improperly, and the resulting explosion, with the aid of super-heated air pockets, opened the earth and left scars on the surface resembling those of mighty Godzilla claws gouging and furrowing the soil. Trees were felled, rocks cracked, and animals scurried from the site with their hair standing straight up and their tails bushed out. This error had to be investigated and the damage assessed. The company geologist, and the company lawyer, working together, followed the gouges to ensure no private property was damaged.

Elijah, the geologist, and Neil, the lawyer, didn't like each other all that much. It wasn't anything said or done that created their mutual animosity. Sometimes a person you meet just rubs you the wrong way. You know you shouldn't judge them, especially since you don't know them, but the old lizard brain told you something was wrong, and you went with it.

Neil said, "How far does this crack go?"

"Maybe a kilometre? Maybe two?"

"That's good. We own twenty square kilometres. Why are we even doing this?"

Elijah said, "You're the lawyer, man. You tell me."

"Right. Liability. Always liability."

Elijah pointed ahead, between a break in the trees, along the furrow the explosion ripped through the ground.

"What's that?"

"I don't know. A box?"

"Half-buried?"

Neil didn't answer. He walked forward, his Blundstone boots squishing in the mud, and he frowned, hoping the filth didn't reach the cuff of his tailored jeans. *Elijah was right. The box is half-buried.*

He heard Elijah's steps behind him. He ploughed ahead, transfixed by the oddity in the earth. He stopped before it and said, "Is that?"

Elijah said, "Yeah."

The dark crate, browned from the damp earth, moldy from the elements, had one broken slat allowing them to see what it hid inside. A decaying man, mouth open in a scream, stared at them with unseeing eyes.

Neil said, "I hope we didn't kill him."

Elijah stared at Neil for a beat or two and said, "Don't be an idiot. Do something useful and call the cops."

•　　•　　•

Forensics officers, detectives, and uniform police officers swarmed the area. The scene was photographed, evidence was collected, statements were taken, and the identity of the killer remained a mystery. The victim was identified as Ken, their missing runner. Now that they had a body, it was a verified homicide and if they caught someone, the defence wouldn't be able to say, 'no body, no homicide'. Which, to be fair, was a good defence. If you can't prove how the person died, you certainly can't point your finger at someone and blame them for what you couldn't prove. Without a body, who could say definitively what happened?

They recovered the mini cameras, photographed the holes for the water hoses and concluded this killer was sophisticated, organized, and would be difficult to catch. Davis would get more pressure from the brass now. He remembered the Jackal and shuddered. And then he remembered Matt and what this would mean to him. Someone would have to tell him, and that someone would be Davis. There were days when he hated his job.

-34-

EDUCATION PART 8

It was better living alone. No one walking around, oozing paranoia from their pores and no scent of the unwashed sweat of the crazy. He enjoyed the solitude. In this time, he created a student ID, enrolled in online courses, and furthered his education. He took courses in finance, law, history and French language lessons. He followed the law courses up with forensic evidence collection and subscribed to a Forensic Sciences online magazine to be kept apprised of new technologies and techniques developed to catch men such as himself. He had the time. From the money his father had invested, now his own, he could live comfortably off the yearly returns. Because of the freedom the money bought for him, he read everything he thought would be beneficial for him to know in pursuit of his passion. Hunting magazines, law and security magazines, fitness and health magazines, and for more cerebral exercises, philosophy.

He hadn't expected to be as engrossed in philosophy as he was. He had been looking for something, anything, that attempted to explain life or the purpose of it. Almost all of the philosophy books he read had in them some useful nuggets to contemplate. He tended to be more drawn to the philosophies that supported his own thoughts on life. He found himself embracing the ideas of existential nihilism, an idea which critics of Hemingway proposed he had explored in his stories. The ideas presented by Nietzsche and the Marquis de Sade intrigued and further reinforced his own beliefs. Life was meaningless. An accident of the cosmos. It was to be enjoyed for its own sake and not for the sake of others. Nothing gave him more joy than the idea of destroying lives that, through a cosmic fluke and the gruelling process of evolution, took millennia to develop. He didn't believe in God. But in taking life, it was the closest thing a person could do to becoming God-like.

• • •

After seeing the news on the TV about the finding of Ken, the killer said, "Fuck."

He never thought luck was a thing. To acknowledge the universe picked favourites, on this tiny little planet out of a gazillion of them, seemed ludicrous in the extreme. Even now, he didn't think he should consider the possibility. Only a small part of him, the kid part of him that still believed in the unbelievable, thought luck just might *be* a thing. Let's consider this past year. His truck (now at the bottom of a lake) was not only seen, but photographed at an abduction site, and then, inexplicably, it was traced back to his home, and even worse, the cops showed up at his house, wanting to speak to him about the truck. Those events were bad enough, but now they found Ken's body because a nickel mine explosion had unearthed it? Unreal.

Barefoot, in shorts and a T-shirt, and a glass of water in his hand, he evaluated his situation. The itch was building. He was ready to take another. He'd refined his chloroform mixture, and he made an awesome little murder toy to amplify his experience. Could he afford to kill again? Now with this added exposure? Not directly at him, but to his activities? He'd had no further visits from the police. No one was watching him that he could tell unless the police were disguised as a hydro pole.

As such, he'd been left alone for the past few months to complete his newest project. Once that was done, he should be able to do whatever he wanted without fear of discovery. He should be good to go. Except for wheels. He needed new wheels. He'd been too busy with the project to look into getting a new truck. The Range Rover was not a car to transport bodies in. Too conspicuous. He missed that old truck of his. Should be easy enough to get a new one. A lot of times, when an adult's parents die, they end up with a lot of stuff they don't want. What do they do? They sell said 'stuff'. He could buy himself a used vehicle owned by the recently deceased and just neglect to register the transfer with the Ministry of Transportation. Or he could make the transfer using one of his identifications. No. Why expose his other IDs if he didn't have to? A vehicle owned by a dead person was better.

To find another vehicle, a blending-into-the-background type of vehicle would take time which would give him more time to refine his new toy. Besides, there was no need to rush. The world teemed with victims. There would never be a shortage.

-35-

During the time before Ken had been found, as the politics of COVID continued to divide people, Bibi and Olivia, met, liked what they saw in each other, and became friends. They started their relationship over the phone, both of them shy, unwilling to peel back their hard shells until the other did it first. They approached each other with trepidation, waiting and expecting for the other person to prove themselves a letdown or a disappointment. When that didn't happen, they moved to Skype calls, and Olivia noticed Bibi liked to use her hands a lot when speaking, punctuating sentences with a flurry of finger moves and wrist rotations. Bibi noticed Olivia kept a lock of her hair down, to cover where her ear had been sawn off. Bibi didn't know about the ear at first and only thought Olivia liked to wear her hair that way. Bibi considered doing the same to her hair. Olivia was having a strong influence on her, and aware of it, she didn't resist the pull because Olivia fuelled her hope. Bibi would remember the first time they met in person for as long as she lived.

It had been in late March. The snow that had accumulated from October of last year until then made no attempts to melt or recede from the driveways they bordered like the walls of a medieval fort. Bibi drove to Olivia's home using Rori's car and parked where she thought the curb might be hidden in the snow outside of Olivia's home. Olivia stood at the bottom of her driveway surrounded by three dogs. One of them sat in a red wagon, and the other two flanked it. All German Shepherds, all eyeing Bibi with the type of indifference only predatory animals possess. Bibi had seen a wolf in the wild once on one of her hikes. Bibi stopped and stood still when she noticed it. Grey fur, yellow eyes, the beast's head would be, Bibi estimated, just under her shoulder. Bibi knew wolves travelled in packs and the hairs stood up all over her body. She only saw one wolf. Where were the others? Surrounding her now? Bibi wanted to turn her head, take in her surroundings, make sure the wolves weren't encircling her, but she couldn't pull her gaze from the wolf. The wild eyes regarded her with indifference. Its reaction would depend on Bibi. If she attacked it or threatened it, the wolf would react. If she did nothing at all, the wolf would do nothing. It didn't care either way. In that instance, Bibi would decide her fate. She stood still, lowered her eyes, and waited. She heard the wolf chuff and when she looked up, it had gone.

Olivia's dogs viewed her in the same way at their first meeting. Bibi was nothing. Not a friend, not a foe, she was nothing until Olivia decided what Bibi would be to them. Olivia was the pack leader.

Bibi walked over to Olivia, hands in her pocket, the self-conscious gait of a teenager approaching someone they liked. As she stepped on the driveway, Olivia embraced her in a hug. She said, "I'm so glad to meet you."

Bibi didn't reply with words. She was too choked up. She returned the embrace.

•　　•　　•

Olivia and Bibi walked the sidewalks and trails surrounding Olivia's neighbourhood. The tires of Brutus' wagon rolled over a thin layer of snow left on the sidewalk after the mini ploughs did their work. New snow hadn't fallen for some time and the snow on the trails had been compressed and hardened with the many trail walkers in the area. Olivia and Bibi walked side by side, dressed for the cold weather with the dogs trailing slowly behind them. Sometimes, Freya or Odin would be distracted by an errant smell and would fall behind, their ears turned to Olivia to keep track of her. Once they satisfied their curiosity, they hurried to catch up to Olivia and Bibi. After the awkwardness of meeting each other in person had vanished, they slid back into the comfortable conversational patterns they established first over the phone and then using FaceTime. Olivia thought their entire friendship interesting. They hadn't known each a long time, but they *knew* each other. Their shared experiences had carved them into people different than who they had been before. The naivety, the youthful optimism had been ripped from them. They knew the darkness of the world. Not in an abstract way, like people talking about violence without any knowledge of it. Olivia knew violence. Bibi knew it too. They understood each other on a level most people would never experience. Like when a war veteran returns home and their friends, family, who never walked in their shoes would ask, "What was it like?" As though there was a language that existed that was adequate enough to describe it. And because it couldn't be described, no one you loved knew what any of it was like. You'd have to live it to understand. Soldiers knew this, and they related to each other in a secret language their family and friends would never comprehend. And Bibi got it. Bibi knew the language. It made their bonding that much faster.

"Did you train them?"

Olivia glanced back at her dogs, her four-legged family, smiled and said, "Yes and no."

"Uh, elaborate please."

Olivia smiled, paused, prepared to tell the story and the smile faded from her face. She said, "After my dad died, I was obviously a mess. I couldn't, can't actually, get over the notion that he died because of me."

Bibi opened her mouth to offer the same bromides as others, but Olivia raised a hand to wave it off and continued, "All I had left to me was Brutus here and for a while, he was enough. I have an uncle, but I don't know, it's hard, he uh, just stopped talking to me or I pushed him away, probably a little bit of both, and other than Davis and Brutus, I had no one. I was alone and afraid. Always afraid. I didn't want to go outside, and I didn't want to stay inside, because of how the Jackal got in, and I don't know, there was like this, this sounds stupid, like a tornado in my head. Fear, guilt, loss, and I don't even know how many other emotions there are, but they were all spinning in my head, all day, all night. I don't think I slept over four hours a night, if that, after my dad died. Fear though, that was the big one. Brutus saved my life that night when the Jackal crept into my room. And I thought, why not have more of him? For me, and for Brutus. Brutus was a rescue dog, but Freya and Odin, I bought them from a training center specializing in security dogs. German Shepherds are fiercely loyal and very protective. I had a personal dog trainer from the center come over five times a week to work me through training them. They're not only my family, they're guard dogs. With a word from me, they'd take down anyone I tell them to. They give me the courage I couldn't manufacture on my own. They're the reason I leave my house now."

"You go out-out?"

"What does that mean?"

"Like to the grocery store? Shopping for clothes? Maybe see a movie?"

Olivia looked at her as if to say, *you crazy?* Olivia said, "There's this thing called the internet, where you can order clothes, food, rent movies-"

"All right, I get it."

A squirrel ran across the trail in front of them. Freya and Odin tensed, looking to Olivia, wanting permission to chase the bushy-tailed creature but Olivia gave no such permission, and they resumed their walk, with their snouts pointing to where the animal had vanished. The landscape, coated in white dust, was still and clean. Bare branches outlined with white ice crystals forming and growing into long knives on their ends, bending them toward the earth with their weight. Plumes of white left their mouths with every exhale. Their feet crunched through the light layer of snow. Brutus' wheels squealed every so often.

Bibi, enjoying the calm, the peace, the rightness of being with someone who understood her, said, "Do you think we'll ever get back to normal?"

Olivia sighed and said, "What's normal? To walk around and pretend that horrors don't exist? That there aren't people out there waiting to do someone, me, you, harm? That's like asking someone who could only see black and white to forget that they had seen colour once."

Olivia pulled out her knife, removing it from the sheath attached to her belt through the hole she had cut in the pocket just for that reason.

Bibi stopped walking. Olivia turned the blade in her hand.

Olivia said, "This is my normal. And there isn't any going back. Not after what I've seen. Not after what I've lived through."

"But the Jackal is dead. Your boogeyman is gone. Doesn't that make things better? Easier?"

"Easier? Maybe. I do feel better knowing he's dead. I'm still scared, but, if he were still out there, I'd probably be a lot worse. But then, Harry would still be alive."

-36-
SPRING OF 2021
EDUCATION PART 9

He remembered the rush, the intensity of the moment when his father murdered the conservation officer. Sadly, the same feeling hadn't been replicated when he murdered his father, and he considered the 'why' afterward. He came to the conclusion that killing his father had been pure business. Even the flaying, which was interesting if not annoying to execute, didn't provoke an emotional response. He wouldn't be honest if the experience (or lack of one) didn't worry him. Had the experience with the conservation officer been so intense it couldn't be repeated ever again? Had he blown his emotional load?

In the refinement of his techniques, hiding and stalking in the woods, he found out early on that wasn't the case. Even the teens catching him hiding in the bush like an idiot didn't diminish the thrill of hunting, stalking and working through in his head how to attack and subdue his prey with brutal efficiency. His first kill, a young man, bound, gagged and helpless. He spent twenty minutes killing him. He'd strangle the man to the point of death and release him. He'd wait until the man had recovered and then do it again. He could have done that over and over all night, but his hands got sore, cramped and by the end, they had stiffened into claws. He resolved to work on his grip strength after that. The man's death had been glorious. If he had tied a weight to his penis, he could've lifted fifty pounds with the strength of his erection. He knew that hunting, stalking, catching and murdering his prey was the only experience he wanted to chase. And most of his energy went into refining how to catch people and experimenting with ways of killing them.

• • •

The killer didn't know the woman he secured to the chair. He never knew any of his victims, not before he'd taken them, and this person was no different. He did, however, find out the name of his victim by going through their pockets, belongings, whatever they had on them, because he liked to disable their phone (everyone had a cell phone nowadays) and he made sure they had no weapons on them. Curiosity would invariably influence him to look at their IDs. He liked having a name for his prey. Better than saying, *"Hey you!"* to get their attention. People responded better to their own name. This time, with this catch, he didn't bother. He liked to think his growing indifference motivated him to lose interest in the name of his prey. Can you be indifferent and motivated? Their being, their person, didn't matter to him. Only their life, and his power of that continuation or termination of their life, mattered. To take a life, to watch the soul (whatever that means) leave the body, to steal from the universe that which it had randomly and without thought had given, well, there was nothing better was there? Satisfied she was secured, he removed her gag.

"What, uh, what is, why can't I move?"

"You're strapped to a chair. I'd find it troubling if you could move."

The woman had short-cropped brown hair. The style you sometimes see new mothers wear because they have enough to do without having to worry about their hair. Her eyes widened as she took in the leather straps binding her wrists to the arms of a heavy wooden chair. She couldn't see what held her legs tight to the chair because her head had been secured to the chair with canvas straps around her forehead, the type movers used with a ratcheting mechanism to tighten them. A strap across her forehead, and another one around her neck. More leather straps bound her shins to the legs of the chair, high enough so her feet couldn't touch the ground. He had her immobilized. The chair was heavy, and he didn't think she'd be able to move it, but it wouldn't do to give her an opportunity to use her feet to push herself back in a panic. Because what he was about to do to her was going to cause an alarm.

Her voice trembled, and she said through chattering teeth, "What do you want?"

He walked toward her and squatted down in front of her. His knees cracked and he winced, thinking he should up his daily dose of collagen pills.

"Before you woke up here, did you see me at all?"

"No."

"So, just walking along a trail, then what?"

"I uh, something was put on my face, something chemically, and then, black. Everything went black."

"You have a headache at all?"

"A little bit."

He studied her, his mouth a straight line, and he nodded. He stood and he walked behind her. She heard him pick up something that clattered, a metallic sound. She swallowed. The strap around her neck made the effort painful. Unable to move her head, her eyes took in her surroundings. A dirt floor stamped flat, dirt walls sheared smooth with pockmarks of where large stones had been, metal support posts holding up metal beams crossing the ceiling, and a generator purring silently with wires running to lights around the room, casting shadows. Against one wall was a workbench, and beside it, a large metal tube, big enough to hold a person, with a metal vent protruding from the top and into the ceiling. Along with the oil smell of the generator was the scent of freshly turned earth. She couldn't see a door, but then, because of her immobility, she couldn't turn her head to view the rest of the room. Underground. She was under the earth with a maniac. He didn't have the wild hair or the scraggly clothes you'd see in a slasher movie, but a maniac all the same. Wearing a splash mask, and a suit you'd see people in biological disaster movies wear. He looked more like a doctor than anything. She blinked back tears and her breath came in rapid inhalations. She couldn't slow her breathing down. Her heart thumped in her chest; her vision starred.

Behind her, she couldn't see what he was doing, but she could hear him, feel him, securing something to the top of her chair. What was he doing?

"Stop, stop, stop, what are you doing? Stop, please stop."

He walked in front of her and petted her hair. He said, "Shhhh. It'll all be over soon."

He returned to his work behind her while his words rang in her head, banging and reverberating like the world's largest gong. *It'll all be over soon.*

She cried. The room blurred.

"There."

He stood in front of her. He held a remote in his hand.

"See this? This is connected to a drill that is above your head. I turn it on with this button, and I make it descend with this button. It descends slowly."

Her mouth hung open, her eyes wide as plates.

"It's okay to scream. No one will hear you."

He pressed one button. The drill spun to life. Putting his face inches from hers, the better to see her eyes, he pressed the second button.

She remained quiet. Not quite believing the madman's words. Just this morning, she was out walking her dog, and now, she was strapped to a chair in an underground lair with a drill poised above her head. This can't be real. Can't be. When the hell would she wake up from this? She asked herself that over and over until the drill bit into the top of her skull. When that happened, she screamed.

•   •   •

His breathing was so rapid, it was as though he had just completed an intense wind sprints workout. He licked the sweat off his upper lip. That had been intense. It took him a minute to realize that she had died and that maybe he should reverse the drill. He did so, and when it came out of the top of her head, the blood and pieces of brain and bone spun from the drill bit. One moment alive, the next; not. No experience existed to rival it.

He walked over to the person-sized metal tube beside his workbench. He turned on the gas and set it alight. He opened the long door, made sure all the burners were lit and closed the door to allow the heat to accumulate. He put a plastic bag over her head and then undid the straps, making sure to do the head last to prevent her from flopping forward when he wasn't ready for it. He undid the last strap from around her head and pulled her from the chair to let her body flop to the floor. Pieces of brain and bone coloured the inside of the bag. He opened the door on the metal tube. He put on heavy, heat-resistant gloves, and then he pulled out the metal gurney guided by rails. Picking her up, he put her on it and arranged her into the fetal position so she'd fit. He put the rest of her belongings on top of her, including her ID. He read her driver's license, finally curious. Her name had been Carmela. He stripped off his splash gear, crumpled it up, and put it on her as well. He pushed the gurney back in and closed the door. He turned the gas to full. It would take three hours at 1600 degrees for the cremation process to be completed. He had built the oven using different parts bought at different stores and knew it worked because he had tested it. He was nothing if not fastidious concerning details. In the meantime, while she was incinerating, he'd clean up the rest of the mess. There was more blood on the chair than he had expected.

If the police and their forensics team got a hold of this chair, he knew they'd be able to recover blood, maybe even enough for a DNA profile. That's not the only reason why he cleaned the chair. He liked a clean workspace. In the end, if the police did find this hidey-hole, he was done for. If they did locate it, after all the pains he'd taken to conceal it, he'd be suitably impressed. The tricky part about this whole place was the ventilation. He had to ventilate the generator fumes and the smoke from the oven. Using various filters and lots and lots of trial and error, he could stand on top of his base of murder without any hint of smoke or escaping vapours. With this setup and his new truck, owned by a dead man, he figured he could go on killing indefinitely. Or at least until age caught up with him. By then, if he couldn't enjoy this one thing he loved, he planned to kill himself. Because, really, what would be the point of continued existence? It's not as if his tiny life on this tiny universal outpost contained any significance.

He thought of the light leaving his latest victim's eyes. What was that? Consciousness? Do all animals have it to some degree? Goddamn that was intense. A shiver ran through him. He grinned. He loved his life.

After the killing room had been cleaned to his satisfaction, he checked on Carmela's progress through the high-temperature window and went to the exit. He ascended a steep set of stairs and pushed on the door above, pressing hard against the steps with his legs to move it. He had placed soil and a layer of sod on top of the trapdoor. The grass took to the dirt with regular watering and after time and care, the grass blended in with the tall wild grass on the ground around the door. A metal handle attached to a short chain allowed him to open it. It had taken a long time to build this during his long hiatus. He had been working on it long before Ken had been found. It had been difficult, especially when it got so cold out the ground froze to a one-foot depth. But with a rented backhoe, it made the job easier. He had been nervous about the police watching him, but they could not watch him without him knowing about it. They'd be too exposed out here. Not that he didn't check outside his house every morning before driving the backhoe out of the garage to his project. It had taken a lot of work but once he had finished it, he wondered why he hadn't thought of this before. Rhetorical notion. He knew why. To have the killing ground on your property put you at risk. To mitigate the risk, he had to make it invisible to all but him. The risks rated low in comparison to the rewards.

He closed the trapdoor behind him and studied the ground. No smoke, no sounds of the generator. He smiled. He nailed this part.

Time to clean out the truck.

He walked to his shed, inhaling the night air on the way, and enjoying the night animals awakening through their cries and the rustling of leaves. He opened the door to his shed, more of a two-car unattached garage, and opened the back door of the four-door pick-up truck. Newer model, a boring white colour, was bought at an auction and still registered to the deceased person who used to own it. It had been harder than he thought to find a suitable vehicle of the recently deceased to buy. The elderly tended to buy Toyota Corollas or Honda Civics rather than pick-up trucks. The auction was the next best option.

He had taken the work chest out of his other truck before driving it into a lake and had installed it in this one. Taking Ken's advice, he cut the sides of the chest so he could lower the end of it, sliding his prey in and out. He released the latches holding the door closed and lowered it, stepping back from it to lay it flat. He blinked.

"What the fuck is this?"

A cell phone sat on the bottom of the chest. He snatched it out and using the swipe-up shortcut, he turned on airplane mode. Sweat broke out all over his body.

"Who the hell carries two cell phones?"

-37-

Her name had been Carmela Montoya and her absence had been noticed immediately. Her morning routine consisted of waking up, getting the kids ready for their online COVID school, and when they had been set up and her husband was off to work, she'd take their dog, Sharpay, out for a walk. Yeah, a stupid name. She regretted allowing the kids the option of naming the dog as soon as they uttered 'Sharpay' from that Disney musical they watched over, and over, and over and over again. She couldn't stand that stupid musical, but a promise was a promise. Their beagle was thus christened Sharpay. And it was Carmela's job to look after it. That's not how it had been initially sold to Carmela by her children. Her husband bought the dog for the kids who said, *please mommy, we'll look after it, we'll walk it, we'll pick up the pooh, we'll feed it, please mommy, please,* and all the while knowing once the kids realized how much work a dog was, especially a puppy, their promises would dry up like vomit in the sun and just as unpleasantly. And funny enough, Carmela ended up loving the little mutt. And the mutt loved her more than anyone else in their family, which Carmela enjoyed with smug satisfaction. Sharpay routinely snubbed and ignored the other family members when she entered the room.

The Montoya's lived in a three-storey home on a half-acre lot. From the back of their property, they could access the public trail which ran for forty kilometres east and twenty-seven kilometres west from their property. On more than one occasion, she had seen ultra-marathon runners using the trail with their camelbacks full of water and their pockets stuffed with treats to eat on their gruelling runs.

It took her five minutes to reach the trail. She checked her watch; 8:50 am. Kids should be busy with their classes now. She decided to head west along the trail for two kilometres and then head back. Her Apple watch would be her distance calculator as it was on most days when she cared to track such things.

She set off at a casual speed, enjoying the white buds on the branches, the bright sun cutting swaths through the morning darkness, and the pockets of stubborn snow still not getting the message that winter had passed and it was time to melt away to return next year. Her eye had been drawn to a tree. The odd shape demanded scrutiny. She squinted at it, and then one of her phones buzzed in her pocket. She pulled it from her pocket and at the same time, the tree moved, crossing the distance to her, and something was pressed against her face. Sharpay barked, and barked and then just like that, blackness.

•　　•　　•

Sharpay nipped at the man-tree's heels, dodging from side to side, barking, protesting against Carmela's treatment. The tree kicked Sharpay. She hit the ground, rolled, and when she rose to her feet, the tree-man and Carmela were gone.

Sharpay ran home and barked, and barked, and barked until Carmela's children let her in. There was no Carmela. They called their dad, who called the police before heading home himself. He thought Carmela might have had an accident on the trail, hurt, maybe unconscious which was why she wasn't answering her phone. Not once did it cross his mind she had been taken. The police checked the trail east and west, looking for anything suspicious since that memo from the detectives had circulated about people going missing on trails. It was understood by every officer and manager that all cases involving a missing person in the woods were to be treated as an abduction until proven otherwise.

Heading west, the officer found a piece of Carmela's phone. He shouldn't have seen it. Fortunately, the waste from two large coffees filled his bladder and he didn't have time to go to the station to use the washroom before he had been dispatched to this call. By the time he reached the trail, he really had to go. Checking the trail behind him, he darted behind a tree, unzipped, freed the mini-him, and was about to spray when the shine of the phone caught his eye.

"Shit."

He couldn't piss on a crime scene. He put himself away, zipped up, and squatted before the phone. The screen had been stomped on. If that wasn't suspicious, he didn't know what was. He called his Sergeant who called others. By noon, the phone calls had made their way to Davis.

-38-

That evening, while search teams scoured the woods in the dark after the Forensics Unit had gathered the requisite evidence, Davis sat in the kitchen of the Montoya's across from Carmela's husband, Gary. Gary's eyes shone, as though shrink-wrapped. They peered at Davis from a puffy face, sullen, sad, and frightened. He kept turning a water bottle on the table with one hand. Davis had spoken to the officer who had initially interviewed Gary and wanted to ask follow-up questions for details that hadn't been acquired.

Davis asked about Carmela's daily routine, her friends, nearby family, her job, and near the end, Gary answered in monosyllables through a tight line of a mouth. He was getting irritated and was too scared and tired to not let it show.

Davis said, "I'm sorry. These questions may not seem important now, but you never know-"

"Can't you guys, like, trace her phone or something? Find out where she is by that, what's it called, triangulation?"

"I don't know if anyone has told you this, but we found her phone, on the trail. It had been damaged."

"Yeah, yeah, I know, but what about her other phone?"

Davis stared.

"Other phone?"

"Yeah. Her other phone! I told the other officer that this morning, hours ago! You mean you guys have done fuck all with it?"

"She has two phones?"

"Are you hard of hearing? Am I fucking stuttering here? Yeah. Her work, Re/Max, gave her a work phone! She has a personal phone and a work phone! One phone plus one phone is guess what, genius? Two fucking phones!"

The blue mask Gary wore over his nose and mouth puffed out with his anger.

"Give me both of her phone numbers."

Gary read off the numbers, arms crossed, eyes fiery orbs.

Davis stood, and Gary said, "If you guys, goddamn, if you guys fucked this up, and Carmela is gone, I'm going for your jobs. Believe it."

Davis said, "I do."

•　　•　　•

Outside, Davis gave the phone numbers to Cam and said, "Start pinging those phones." To Stacy, he said, "Find out who was the first officer to speak to Gary. And from there, find out if he told anyone about Carmela having two phones."

"And then what?"

"I don't know. See what we get from the ping and go from there."

•　　•　　•

When the police have reason to believe a person is in imminent danger, to themselves or from someone else, they can request the phone company send out a ping to that number. If the phone is on, the phone company, depending on the reception area, can get a location on the phone. The accuracy of the location is in direct proportion to the reception area. Davis had seen the ping be accurate to within a three-metre radius. Other times, the result had been within a four-kilometre radius.

The ping on Carmela's work phone, the one left in the truck of the killer, returned a three-hundred metre radius of where the phone would be. Plugging the coordinates given into Google maps, they zoomed in on the area in question.

Stacy said, "Will you look at that."

Davis said, "What am I looking at?"

"That, my good Sergeant, is right near where our friend-who-wouldn't-identify-himself lives."

"Walt Griffin?"

"That's right."

"When you say right near, what does that mean? It looks to me like it's right on the house and garage there."

"Three-hundred metre radius, remember? Half the circle is on the property and the other half, isn't."

"Ok. Let's get Tac and K-9 rolling, like right now."

Cam said, "No K-9 available. All the dogs are up north on that drug-lab-take-down-thingy."

"We have Tac, though, right?"

"Not a full team."

"Great. Fill up the rest of the spots with any available uniform officers, and Cam?"

"Yeah."

"Have dispatch keep pinging the phone, see if we can get a tighter radius."

"They've been doing that. I told them to keep doing that in case the phone moves."

"Good idea."

"Yeah. I thought so. Except now the phone is either off or in airplane mode. Either way, no more pings."

"Fuck it. That's good enough for me. Let's get going."

-39-
EDUCATION PART 10

There were two reasons why he used different techniques to kill his prey. Number one: to never be tied to a certain killing style. If he always stabbed someone in the chest and sliced up their face, and if any of his victims had been found, he wouldn't want them associated with a single killer. Number two: their fear. Increasing the fear of his prey became another evolving aspect of his passionate pursuit. He spent hours ruminating on how to accomplish the most fear prior to death. To satisfy his requirements, the prey had to die relatively quickly. He couldn't risk playing around with them in the woods or elsewhere for long periods of time. The odds of someone stumbling upon him were ridiculously low. Staying too long in one area increased the risk of being found or 'caught red-handed' as they say. With every experiment, there existed the potential for failure.

One young woman he had secured to the ground, staked out, gagged and in that state of fear he sought and loved when he stimulated it, ready for the coup de grace and after theatrically displaying how she would die to increase her terror, he set off the mechanism and... nothing.

Using counterweights, rope, and a sharpened stake, he had devised an interesting kill-trap. Simple to execute, the trap would drop the sharpened stake and with the counterweights, it should pierce the chest and pin the victim to the ground like a bug. All he had to do was cut a rope holding the weights. Not realizing it at the time, when setting up the counterweights, he had tied them generously to make sure they would hold. In this generous tie, he had wrapped the rope around a thick branch. When he cut the rope, the weights didn't fall, and the stake stayed where it was up above them promising menace but delivering confusion. In the end, he used his knife to cut her throat. A disappointment for sure, but there were plenty of 'victims' in the sea, and he had plenty of time.

•　　•　　•

The killer assumed the police were on their way. Or were they already here?

He ran to his house, went in through the back door, and rushed to the front window. No approaching car lights, nothing. Ok. That's good, that means he has time. Better not waste it.

He picked up a flashlight from the garage and sprinted to his killing room. He tugged on the chain, the door opened, and he dropped down into the hole, foregoing using the stairs. He picked up his heavy gloves, opened the door on the homemade incinerator, making sure to keep the door between him and the escaping heat, and he tossed the phone inside. He closed the door and checked his watch. She'd only been in there for forty-five minutes. Three more hours and she'd be dust. He needed the cops off his property as soon as possible. Were they coming to arrest him? A thrill of fear pulsed through his veins. He'd worry about that if it happened. For now, he could leave the incinerator going, and the generator. He didn't fear either one would cause a fire as both would time out after four hours of use. He left the room and closed the hidden door. He ran back to the garage, really starting to sweat out here (and that's another thing he needs to think about before the cops arrive because a sweaty man always looked like a guilty man), and he tossed all the tools lying about into the work chest in the back of the pick-up, thinking *hurry, hurry, they're coming…* and there, done. He clicked the button to lock the chest.

He left the garage and ran into the house. He turned on the shower, stripped off his clothes, and hopped in. He soaped up fast, rinsed, hopped out, dried, and dressed in clean clothes. Looking in the mirror, he noticed a wildness in his eyes. *Calm down man. You have time. Think it through.* He combed his hair and styled his beard.

What can the cops do? If they think the phone is here, no way would they wait for a warrant. They could enter onto his property using what lawyers called 'exigent circumstances'. That being said, they could only look for the person they think the phone belongs to. They couldn't tear his house apart and do a complete search without a warrant. Exigency only stretched the courts' tolerance to an invasion of privacy so far. They could only look in places where a person could conceivably be hidden.

And they could arrest him, hold him for investigative detention, depending on what other evidence they had. If he was arrested, they wouldn't release him unless they were satisfied that he is who he says he is. Identity is a primary component when releasing people from custody. What ID would be most appropriate? The house is registered to Walt Griffin. The Range Rover is registered to Walt Griffin. The pick-up truck is registered to Victor Crawley, a dead man. That could be a problem. In the end, he removed his Walt Griffin ID from his safe hidden in the floor under the carpet in his bedroom closet. He'd deal with who owns the truck when he has to. He rolled the carpet back in place, tucked the carpet ends under the baseboard, measured how natural it looked, nodded, and flinched when the doorbell rang. Time to turn on his Meryl Streep. What if they had brought K-9? Would it be able to pick up Carmela's scent? Teasing fingers of fear caressed his bowels. He answered the door.

-40-

The door was opened by a man with a groomed hipster beard and hair parted to the left with the part so perfect, the white skin glowed beside the dark, oiled hair. Davis moved from behind the Tac officers in all their gear to stand in front of the man.

Davis said, "Walt Griffin?"

"Yes."

"I'm detective Davis with the Ontario Provincial Police. I'm investigating an abduction and we tracked the victim's phone to this address."

The man's eyebrows rose to his hairline, "Here?"

"Yes."

"That's impossible."

"Impossible or not, we have to do a search of the property, to ensure the person is not here. And can you open the gate at the end of the driveway? There are a lot of cars parked on the road."

"Sure. I can do that." Walt leaned back, and his hand moved to the wall on the inside of the house to what Davis assumed to be a button. The gate swung open. More vehicles swept in.

"While the officers search the premises, I'd like you to come with me to the nearest station, where we can conduct an interview."

Walt stepped aside as the Tactical officers walked into the home. Stacy stood beside Davis. Cameron and Brandon followed the Tactical officers inside.

Walter frowned, said, "Am I under arrest?"

"You're being investigatively detained."

"What does that mean for me? Do I have a choice?"

"To a certain degree. You don't have to come with us to the station, but at the same time, you're not free to leave or go anywhere without a police presence.

I could handcuff you, if I thought you posed a risk to me or other officers or if I thought you'd interfere with the search in any way."

"So, I don't have to go with you?"

"No. Well, hold on that."

Davis stepped away and motioned for Stacy to follow. Davis said, "Can you have Cam and Brandon go with one of the Tac guys to see if that blue truck is in the garage?"

Stacy nodded and walked past Walt to go inside.

Walt said, "Well?"

"I don't know yet."

Walt frowned, "That was an unexpected answer."

"Yeah. For me, too."

Stacy returned a short time later from the side of the house. Davis turned to her, she shook her head, and he said to Walt, "No. You don't have to come with us. Not yet anyway. We still have to do a sweep of your property. And while we're here, I'd like to ask you some questions."

Walt hadn't noticed a police dog or heard one barking. His confidence increased, and his manner became more relaxed. He said, "Ok. In that case, would you like to come in, sit at the table? I can offer you a coffee or tea, or a diet soda. That's all I have."

Davis said, "I'm fine for now. The table would be great though."

"Follow me."

Walt turned his back and Davis noticed the sloping muscular shoulders under the oversized large sweatshirt. Walt wore clothes like some people who are overweight wear their clothes; over large to hide their body. Walt was not overweight. He appeared fit and strong and Davis wondered why a person would want to hide that. To appear less menacing? To gain trust? Or was he attributing motives to someone he didn't know?

He followed Walt through a living room of powder blue walls and IKEA efficient furniture and shelves. Davis stopped before the bookshelf and glanced at the titles. Canadian Criminal Code, Major Case Management Manual, Forensic Evidence Processing, The Intelligent Investor, and various titles on the topic of investing, astronomy, and classical literature.

"This way, detective."

Davis turned to Walt, smiled and walked toward him.

The slate grey table was surrounded by four black chairs. These items were decidedly not from IKEA.

Walt sat on a chair with his back to a door. Davis, before sitting, removed his cell phone from his pocket. He put a large notebook on the table.

"There is a police application on my phone that allows me to audio and video record interviews. I'm going to turn this on before I begin with questions, to make sure most of our interaction is recorded, for integrity purposes."

Walt nodded.

Davis said, "Stacy, you wanna record this please?"

"You bet."

He gave Stacy his phone, watched her as she fiddled with it, and while looking at the screen, said to Davis, "Ready when you are."

"Ok. Let's start."

When the recording started, Davis introduced himself, Walt, Stacy, and then stated where they were at the present date and time.

Davis said, "We're investigating an abduction. The phone belonging to the abducted person was pinged to get the location of the phone, and hopefully, find the victim. The location returned was here, on your property. And that's why we're here, and why we are detaining you pending the search of your property. Before we begin, I have to let you know you don't have to say anything to the police about this. Anything you do say will be recorded and may be used at a trial against you. You may talk to a lawyer. One of your choice, or if you don't have one, we can provide you with one for free legal advice. Do you wish to speak with a lawyer?"

Walt paused, arms folded across his chest, said, "No."

Davis noticed the powerful frame underneath the baggy sweater. A strong man like him could pull or carry a man through the snow to a truck hidden behind an out-of-business diner.

"Can you tell me what you were doing from the time you got up until the time that the police knocked on your door?"

"I gather, from your first statement, the caution, that I don't have to answer any questions?"

"That's correct."

Walt nodded, said, "Might as well let you know then, I'm not going to answer any question you ask me. Not one. I've confirmed my name, and you know my address, and I believe that is all I have to tell you, correct?"

"That's correct."

"Now, I have a large property, and it might take some time for your search team to finish… searching. So would you like a coffee while you wait? I'd like to make one if that's ok."

"No. Thank you. If I may ask, why won't you talk to the police? If you've done nothing wrong, what could it hurt?"

Walt stood, opened a cupboard and removed a Keurig pod. While getting his coffee ready, he said, "Probably nothing, but probably isn't one hundred percent. And, really, since I've done nothing wrong and I'm not involved, that would imply I have no helpful information because I have no knowledge of this crime."

"It would help us rule you out."

"Would it? I wonder. And why would that matter to me? Me making your job easier?"

Walt filled the Keurig with water, placed the pod inside and closed the lid. The white mug had a cartoon sloth on it hanging from a tree.

"The phone drew us here, but we have wanted to talk to you before, concerning another abduction investigation, and you didn't want to talk to us then either."

Walt, leaned back against the counter with his hands splayed out to the side, fingers gripping the countertop as though he could snap it off. His body didn't relay the tension indicating he would crack it, but the power in his frame and his stance suggested violence barely tamed. Walt didn't answer Davis. Walt shrugged, a 'so what' gesture, his face relaxed with a gleam of amusement lighting his eyes.

"A blue pickup, distinctive, had been seen at the site of an attempted abduction five years ago, and the same truck, not too long ago, was captured in a photograph at the site of another abduction. Weird right? Five years apart, same truck. Yeah. I'd say that's weird. And we wouldn't have even known the connection if it hadn't been for Bibi Khan. The one who got away. The one who slipped through the maniac's clumsy fingers."

Walt didn't move, didn't even turn as the machine notified him with a beep that his coffee was ready. The amusement left his eyes. His jaw bulged. Davis thought, *there he is.*

"And that same truck was parked right here, right in that garage outside not too long ago."

Walt waited, squeezed the counter with his hands, and pushed off and turned to pick up his coffee cup. He brought the drink to the table and sat down.

"I don't have a blue pickup. I never had one."

"Sure. Do you know Bibi Khan?"

Walt sipped his coffee, smiled and made an exaggerated 'ah' sound, to mark his appreciation of the dark liquid. He put the coffee cup on the table.

"How about Ken Vega?"

No answer.

"Carmela Montoya?"

No answer yet again.

"How do you suppose Carmela's phone ended up on your property?"

"You really should try this coffee. A Cuban bean, dark roast, extra bitter. The caffeine in it could fuel the Canadian Olympic sprint team."

•　　•　　•

The search yielded nothing. They continued to ping the phone but hadn't received a signal for hours which prevented them from obtaining a smaller search radius. They searched the house, the garage, and the interior of his fenced-in property. They ran the plates on the truck and the Range Rover. The Rover was registered to Walt and the truck was not. He wouldn't answer any questions about the truck either. Since the truck was on private property and not listed as stolen, he didn't have to answer any questions about it, and he knew it.

Davis and Stacy were the last to leave. Davis squeezed the keys in his hand. His jaw bulged, and he turned back and looked at the house. Walt watched him from the open front door.

He tossed Stacy the keys and said, "You're driving."

He got in the passenger side. Stacy started the car. Through the windshield, Davis watched Walt leaning against the frame of his open front door with his arms crossed yet again.

Davis said, "Motherfucker."

Stacy: "This doesn't feel right. She's here. Carmela is here, man."

"Yeah. Maybe. Either way, he knows where she is. I'd bet my left nut on it."

"Gross. Why do guys always bet their left nut? Why not the right?"

Davis wasn't in the mood. He said, "Let's go. We gotta figure out how to nail this fucker. We gotta stop him. First, we'll do a deep, deep, dive into who this guy is. Where did he go to school? Does he have any friends? Where does he work? After we're done with him, a fisting would feel less intrusive. And then, we gotta watch this guy. All the time. If we can't nail him, we have to at least stop him from killing again."

Stacy said, "Do you think she's alive right now? Carmela? Waiting somewhere in the dark, tied up, hoping for us to find her?"

"I don't know. Maybe. Fuck. No. I think she's gone. He seemed too cool, too calm."

"Yeah."

Thinking of the officer who didn't tell him or any of the investigators about Carmela's second phone, Davis said, "But she didn't have to be."

-41-

Davis fought the impossible fight. Administrators, department lawyers, and even the city council weighed in on the surveillance issue. Davis did not consider himself a cynical person. He had always let the political nonsense fall off his shoulders without harm to his essential self. In policing, you had to develop thick skin. Almost no one was happy to see you. People called the police, for the most part, because they needed help at their worst moments. Sure, you got the 'why the hell are you calling police?' incidents when someone wasn't happy with their order at Burger King, but those type of calls were not typical. Police were asked to invade intimate parts of people's lives and were resented, even hated, for doing so. It wasn't uncommon to be called racist (if you were white), Uncle Tom (if you were black) or any other derogatory term in the hopes of delegitimizing the police's authority. Police officers definitely fucked up. They are human after all. What the public fails to understand at times is that the police officers who care, who have integrity, would love for those other assholes to go away. One bad piece of fruit can ruin the batch by association. Essentially, as a cop, you have to be professional, and recognize that when people say they hate you, they mean the uniform and what that represents, and not you personally, which are two totally different concepts.

Politics though, was a different beast entirely. A short-sighted beast. A paranoid beast only concerned with 'optics' as opposed to doing the best for the people who put their trust in them. And shit tended to roll downhill. The city got the bill for the three weeks of surveillance, they threw up their arms, called the Chief, who called the Inspector, who called Davis' Inspector, who of course, called Davis into her office. Davis liked his Inspector. She was a no-nonsense investigator, diligent, honest and her integrity was stellar. Questioning him, in her office, she appeared almost embarrassed.

"What do you have? Help me out here. How can we continue justifying this expense?"

Davis said, "If we don't continue this, someone will die. That's the justification."

"How do you know that? Can you prove it?"

"C'mon, Inspector, if I could prove anything he'd be under arrest. We got the tracking warrant. It's good for sixty days, let's ride that out at least."

"Sixty days of overtime?"

"I know. But I know for a fact that the longer we watch this asshole, pin him in his home, we'll be saving someone's life." She opened her mouth, and he waved his hands and continued, "Yeah, yeah, I know that sounds melodramatic, but that doesn't make it any less true. And maybe, maybe we could catch ourselves a serial killer. And put that asshole away for as long as the courts allow."

"I know you. And because of that, I believe you. But this can't go on indefinitely. One more week. Then I'll have Intel only surveil him during their normal working hours. No overtime."

"What if-"

"You have the tracking devices, right? If he moves, we could have Intel out within an hour."

"It takes a lot less time than an hour to kill someone."

"Enough. That's the plan. That's what we're doing. Deal with it, and plan accordingly."

●　　●　　●

It pissed him off. And when the anger subsided to a degree in which he could ponder the situation in a detached manner, he was rocked loose when he thought of Olivia. He'd failed her. Again. Another killer walking free. And it shamed him, and so he thought, for his sake and hers (mostly his), he should let her know. He knew she'd tell Bibi and then maybe, he wouldn't have to be exposed to Bibi's wrath. Maybe, Olivia would soften the news for him. And he wouldn't have to face Bibi and read his failure in her eyes too. God, he was such a coward sometimes.

-42-

Davis brought Great Canadian Bagel sandwiches, a diet cherry Coke for him, and a diet vanilla Coke to Olivia's house for lunch. When he arrived, he walked to her door, knocked, got no answer and texted Olivia asking her where she was and she texted back, *5 minutes out, relax you sandwich bully.*

He smiled, put the drinks and the bag with their sandwiches inside down on the porch, and sat, waiting for her. The spring sun with no breeze carrying the memory of winter to soften the heat drew beads of sweat from Davis' hairline. He took off his coat and blinked. Out of sight, he heard the familiar sound of Brutus' wheels on his chair wagon approaching. Squeak, rumble, rumble, squeak, rumble, rumble and Olivia and her four-legged family came into sight on the driveway. He stood.

Olivia smiling as she closed the distance, said, "Not that I'm not happy to see you, but you don't make lunchtime visits unless there is a problem."

"I wanted to see you, see how you're doing, wondering how you and Bibi are getting along…"

Olivia stopped before him, raising her eyebrows. Freya and Odin sat beside her. Brutus rolled toward Davis. His tongue reached out and touched Davis' hand, giving him permission to commence petting. Davis complied, and said, "I might vent a little. If that's ok."

"I don't mind a little venting now and then. Help me get Brutus inside."

"You bet."

•　　•　　•

They ate, drank and talked. A beam of sunlight moved across the table, a sundial of sorts, marking their time. Olivia described her friendship with Bibi. Davis was happy for her, for them, and when envy began to colour his thoughts, he pushed it away, imagining an ethereal hand swatting the feeling aside with annoyance. He listened, talked and watched. He could see the impact Bibi was having on her. The veil of sadness covering her from head to foot had lost its opaqueness. Hope fluttered there. And Bibi had given it to her. Not him.

Olivia said, "Your interrogation is now over, detective. It's my turn. And my curiosity has yet to be sated. Now, spill it. What did you want to vent about?"

"They are going to pull the surveillance. The tracking device they stuck on both of his vehicles hasn't moved. Not once."

Davis met with or talked with Olivia on a regular basis. He had disclosed to her the problems with the case and Davis' belief that Walt was involved. Although the police never had the evidence to support a warrant to search the property, a tracking warrant did not require the stringent parameters of a warrant to search. Most warrants as written in the Criminal Code of Canada had to be approved by a Justice of the Peace or Judge. Some warrants were Judge only approved, but in order for the warrant to be signed, you had to have evidence to support that reasonable grounds existed that an offence took place and that what you were doing, and what you were after, evidence-wise, was Charter (constitutionally) compliant. A tracking warrant only needed to meet the threshold of reasonable suspicion: a much lower bar to meet. Because the home was in a position in which static surveillance would be all but impossible, a tracking warrant on the vehicles would alert the nearby surveillance team when one of the vehicles was on the move, and they'd be able to follow it electronically and the old-fashioned way, by car. The surveillance had been ongoing for six weeks now and nothing had come of it. And twenty-four-hour surveillance was exorbitantly expensive. The administrators who approved the surveillance had to weigh the risk to the public versus the cost to the public. Most times, money would win. It had a way of making people rationalize foolish decisions. Olivia knew all this from Davis and her own personal experience. Unknown to Davis, which Olivia felt a twinge of guilt for now and then, she shared his information with Bibi. The idea another Jackal or Gorilla could be operating out there had kept her up at night. Telling what she knew to Bibi lessened the impact somehow, sharing the burden with someone who knew that real monsters did exist. And this was Bibi's monster after all. This time, what Davis had to say was too much. The police were quitting again. And before they got their act together, someone else would have to die.

Olivia put down her drink without taking a sip.

"It's happening again, isn't it?"

"What?" Her question stunned him, temporarily forgetting the parallels between this case and what had happened to her. They hadn't known who the Jackal was so the police had been watching her, not the bad guy, so maybe that was why the connection didn't appear obvious at first.

Olivia ran her fingers over the scar of her missing ear. She said, more to herself than Davis, "Is he holding them in rooms, rooms like mine? Or cages? And what is he doing to them, you think? Is he cutting parts off of them? Taking pleasure in their hopeless and helpless situation? Were those people waiting for someone to help them and had that hope been carved from them with a knife? Or a razor? Maybe even garden shears."

She stood and paced the short distance from her kitchen back to the table. Brutus whined. Freya and Odin left their mats to watch her, their tails stiff as wooden boards.

Davis wanting to lessen the comparison between her case and this one said, "I think he kills them. And then disposes of them in a way they'll never be found. With Ken, it was lucky he'd been found at all. A mine explosion exposed him."

"But you don't know that's he's not holding them or others right now."

"No. I don't know for sure."

"Then they could be out there. Alive. And their version of Harry is waiting for them to come home."

•   •   •

On the return drive to the office, Davis' mind didn't notice the traffic around him or the noises spilling out of the car speakers. They were there, on the outskirts, like the background of a picture just out of focus, only his mind replayed Olivia's distraught frame moving back and forth with eyes shiny as a fresh coat of paint. Why did he think he could talk to her like that? How irresponsible could he be? After all she's been through, a friend wouldn't drive over and submerge her back into the dark mud from which she had fought to free herself. Why did he do that? *Because she brings you comfort.* He knew the thought to be true and it filled him with shame. His needs trumped her vulnerability. He was hurting her. What an asshole friend he was. He exhaled. From now on, no more investigative talk with Olivia. And this time, he meant to keep the promise to himself.

-43-

Bibi's transformation as a result of her friendship with Olivia was startling. She had moved out of her friend's place into an apartment of her own, a place with surveillance cameras in not-too-hidden white domes on the ceiling, and tenants who were all on the same page about their safety. No one let anyone into the apartment building they didn't know. Period. Pizza guy? Too bad. Ring the right apartment buzzer. You say you're visiting a friend in apartment 312? Call them and have them let you in because if I don't know you, you need to get lost. Bibi approved of the adherence to community safety and security. She finally allowed normalcy to return to her life. Somewhat. Now, she wore a knife on her belt, like Olivia, and had purchased (illegally from an American shipper) a stun gun to carry in another pocket. She had even cut a hole in a couple of her coats so she could reach the handle of the knife from inside, just like Olivia. She even considered getting a guard dog of her own and after some thought, or what hippies might call 'soul searching' she dismissed the idea for two reasons. One: she didn't want anything depending on her. Two: walking a dog would make her predictable. You have to walk your dog. Usually in the morning and in the evening. Anyone watching her would know what time she would be out of the apartment and they would know when to set up an ambush. It had been five years and the woodsman still hadn't come for her. And yeah, maybe she was paranoid to always act as if he was one bad mood away from coming for her, for revenge. That still didn't make the possibility less real or less frightening. Why set up a routine to make it easier for him? Or anyone for that matter?

Bibi, taking a break from her latest freelancing project, stood at her fourth-floor apartment window, watching the evening traffic of people returning home from wherever they had been. A man held the hand of a small child as they crossed the lot. An older woman pushing a walker, her back bent forward as flat as a table with bags of groceries rubbing against the tires, made her way determinedly to the front of the building. The setting sun blinked on windshields and the reflection of white clouds was caught on the shiny roofs of parked cars. Bibi touched the handle of the knife on her belt, not realizing she'd seen Olivia do the same thing during their many meetups. The touch of the handle brought back snippets, photographs in her mind, of the woodsman. And she remembered her conversation with Olivia about him.

Olivia said the police knew who the woodsman was.

Olivia said the police were doing surveillance on him.

Olivia said they would get him soon.

She had learned the information as they walked Olivia's dogs on the gravel trails around Olivia's home, trees standing at attention along the boundaries, their spring buds dropping white petals on the soft earth. They had stopped because Odin had taken an interest in a branch on the ground and was deciding whether to let the other dogs in the area know he'd been there by urinating on it. They were face to face and when Olivia said the last bit, how the cops would get him soon, her eyes slid from Bibi's and found new interest elsewhere and Bibi saw it for what it was. Self-deception. Olivia wanted it to be true. Her insides told her something different. She had experience with the police from her own case. Even though they were well-intentioned, they were hampered. With politics, the Charter, whatever, they were hampered. And Olivia, because of her friendship with Davis, *wanted* the lie to be true.

It took Bibi some time to process the proffered update on the investigation. She thought about it while eating dinner in front of the TV, seeing and hearing the show, but not paying any attention to it. Her mind churned over the police's impotence and what that meant for her. Her anger developed into a rage, and all she could think about was the woodsman, waiting out the police, biding his time, so he could kill again. She rubbed at her wrists, ghosts of the binds he had trapped her with itching from five years ago. A lot of times, victims remain victims because they wait. Wait for the system to do what it says it will do: to obtain justice in a cold and impartial manner. 'Believe in us' the judges said. What did those robed assholes know of fear? Of pain? Of the absolute certainty that a man held your life in his hands and only his short inattention had allowed you the opportunity to save yourself? They knew nothing but, at the same time, purported to know what was best for everyone. The arrogance of it took her breath away. She jumped when her phone buzzed in her pocket.

"Hey, Olivia."

"Bibi."

Bibi heard something in her voice. She said, "You okay?"

"I don't know. Uh, no. I'm not."

"You want me to come over? I'll take an Uber."

"Wait. I have to tell you something."

"What?"

Olivia's confused calm broke, "The cops! The fucking cops! They're doing it again! Over money! They're doing it all over again!"

"What? What are you talking about?"

"They're pulling the surveillance. They've got nothing and they're giving up. Because it's fucking costing them too much money!"

Bibi heard a click in her skull. Her back tooth moved in its gums. She had been grinding her teeth so hard she'd loosened one of them. Blood pulsed in her eyeballs.

Bibi said, "I'm coming over."

• • •

Freya, Odin, and Brutus were happy to see Bibi. Brutus whined from his plush bed, and Freya and Odin cleaned the floor with their tails. They would never rush to Bibi without Olivia's permission. Olivia, who loved Bibi as another survivor of horrific events, and as a friend, met her with wringing hands.

It didn't take long for Olivia to update Bibi on the status of the investigation, and what Davis had said to her. By the end of the short narrative, Olivia punctuated the incompetence of the police with a generous dose of expletives.

Bibi, sitting at the table said, "Do you drink?"

"No. My dad had a habit. No. I don't drink."

Bibi smiled and shook her head, "I could do anything right now that would help take the edge off. That's so not like me."

Bibi rocked back and forth, her jaw flexed, her eyes fixated on a spot on the floor. Her fingers groped for the knife handle on her waist.

Bibi said, "We have to stop him."

Olivia said, "I know."

-44-
EDUCATION PART 11

He had never been socialized. He knew it. And he knew it made him awkward. He didn't know how to start conversations. He didn't understand simple social cues. He didn't leave his home often enough for it to matter and didn't want to spend too much time on something that wouldn't help him in the end. In the early days, before online shopping became a viable way to obtain your goods, he had to do what the rest of the world had done. Gone shopping.

In the local Wal-Mart, purchasing food and household essentials and interacting with the staff made him aware of his social shortcomings. He didn't want to be awkward. He didn't want to be different. Weirdness was remembered. When out in the world, out beyond the boundaries of his home, he wanted to be unremarkable. No one remembered the man in the too baggy clothes going about his business, nodding to the right person, and smiling to others. He didn't want to fit in, exactly. He wanted to blend in. He wanted to be seen but not seen at the same time. He wanted to be the baby blue painted wall that no one spent time to look at or examine. He did what he always did when he wanted to accomplish something. He studied the theory and worked on the practical application.

He watched every genre of movie to help him learn how people interact with each other. When was it appropriate to smile? To shake a hand? To utter a friendly hello? He read books on body language. He read books on spy theory (believing they would know best how not to be noticed, how not to stand out). He worked on it. And when he went out into the world, he practiced it. When COVID hit, he no longer had to leave his house. The government actually encouraged him not to. And he sometimes wondered if he had wasted all those hours in trying to learn how to be unnoticed.

• • •

The killer assumed he was being watched. The detective who questioned him had the look of, say, a hunter. Someone like him. They recognized each other right away and circled each other warily with words the way boxers stalked each other in the ring with their hands raised.

For the time being, he had to stop. No more killing. He could wait out the police. He knew they wouldn't be able to watch him forever. It would be too expensive. In the meantime, he knew how to keep himself busy.

Five in the morning, he'd wake up. He'd drink a cup of coffee while staring out his front window, or sitting in the chair by the window, reading the latest topic capturing his interest or, if the mood struck him, enjoying a mini cigar outside at the back of his house. Once done, he'd check on the stock market, manage his investments, pay bills, and then read the news online while eating his pre-workout meal of oatmeal cooked with protein powder, cashew milk and stevia, and when he felt a little daring, a dash or two of cinnamon. Once eaten, he'd do a simple yoga routine to warm up and to allow his body time to digest the complex carbohydrates. Then he'd kick his own ass with a workout. Kettlebells, hitting a rubber tire with a sledgehammer, medicine ball tosses, powerlifting, weighted sled pulls and sprints. His workouts lasted ninety minutes. And if at the end, he hadn't fought off the urge to spill his breakfast contents onto the mat, he didn't think he'd worked hard enough. Sweat covered his entire body, soaking through his clothing. He stripped naked while on the mat, tossed his clothes into the washer, and drank a pre-mixed concoction of electrolytes, amino acids, and essential salts. In the basement he had converted to a gym, stood a large floor freezer filled with cold water. He opened the lid and using a step stool, climbed into the water and submerged himself to his neck. He set the timer on his watch for four minutes. He meditated until his alarm chimed. He exited the bath, towelled off, and took a hot shower to remove the chill. He hated the ice bath. But because he hated it, he forced himself to do it.

He ate a large lunch and took a timed twenty-minute nap in the complete darkness of his bedroom. After the nap and with a large cup of coffee beside him, he sketched out his next murder device. He'd been reading a lot about ancient torture methods and although crude, he thought with a little ingenuity, he could modernize them, refine them into something truly sublime. And he had the perfect room to build it in.

Later, he would have dinner, have one IPA, and read something edifying before damaging his brain with the lures of TV programming. Hell's Kitchen was one of his favourites. He pushed the thought of the police out of his mind. They didn't matter. They could watch him all they wanted. They wouldn't see much. He didn't have to leave his house. He had food, vitamins, clothing, whatever he wanted, delivered to his home. He didn't have to use the PO Box. He used the cards under Walt Griffin's name because if his purchases were being monitored, that's the name the police had for him.

And when he did go outside, he never went toward his killing room. He walked to his garage or walked along his fence line to ensure no portion needed repairing. He could outwait the police like this indefinitely.

Sometimes in the evening, the wanting to kill pushed at him the way an empty needle reminded a junkie that they hadn't had a fix in some time. He let the sensation flutter through him as he examined it. Was killing something he would always have to do? And if that were true, would continuing to live here be the smart thing to do? The police were watching and even though he knew they couldn't watch him forever, anytime someone went missing, they'd be back at his doorstep wanting to ask a few more questions, and then more questions, and they might even build themselves an office across the street from him, just to save themselves driving time.

The further vexing problem had been the sequence of events leading to his discovery. Bibi escaped five years ago. Okay, not a big deal. Sometimes events happened. Learn from them and move forward. And then Ken's body had been discovered as the result of a bizarre circumstance. And because Bibi had escaped, she could identify the pick-up truck seen on the day of Ken's disappearance that had somehow been linked to him. The cherry on top of this disaster sundae had been Carmela's second phone. Bringing the police not only to his doorstep but into his home as well. If he believed in something as stupid as luck, he would think the universe had been conspiring against him. He didn't believe in luck. If someone were to do something this dangerous and illegal for long enough, they were bound to encounter inexplicable setbacks. It might be time to go somewhere new and be someone new.

Why did he have all those IDs if he wouldn't use them? He could disappear, pop up in another province under another name, and continue. He could do his day-trading anywhere, and with his investments and owned property, he didn't have to do that anymore if he didn't want to. He could comfortably live off the interest while investing more at the same time. The idea took route in his brain. He sat at his computer and started researching the other provinces.

Quebec has the most land covered in forests. British Colombia has a lot too, but not near what Quebec has. And where there are forests, there are provincial parks, and of course, people. He'd have to sharpen up his French-speaking, but that would be fun, almost an adventure in itself. His mind flashed to his killing room. He'd grown attached to it. A lot of work had gone into it, and so far, he'd only used it for one kill. A pang of remorse, of loss, twitched within at the thought of filling it all back in with dirt and gravel. It'd been hard work hollowing the area out, making it structurally sound, setting up the makeshift crematorium, and moving a large portion of his tools out there.

He could build another one. An improved version. He had learned a lot from this build. He'd mostly learned what not to do. Moving became more attractive the more he thought about it. Move somewhere new, build a new killing room, become someone new, and start killing people who spoke a whole new language. He smiled. From what he read about the police's Major Case Management protocol; it was only operational in Ontario. In Quebec, they wouldn't be prepared for a predator like him. They wouldn't even see him coming. He could kill, and kill, and kill until he was an evil old man.

He smiled at the thought. He didn't believe in evil. People, situations, and events are what they are. Only a sentient being gives those any value. Evil as a concept, as an entity or force of nature, never made sense to him. But, thinking to himself about his nature, he was knowingly killing people for his own nihilistic there-is-no-meaning-everything-is-meaningless-except-for-personal-experiences-purposes, that can't, by definition be shared. If killing was evil, and his intention was to kill, did that not make him evil? He shook his head. Stupidly simple. For that to be true, he would need to agree to that definition of evil. And killing wasn't evil. It wasn't anything at all.

-45-

"We're not going to kill him."

Olivia said it to outline what she was willing to do. Bibi's intensity had caused her concern and she wanted it laid out right at the beginning what was acceptable. They had been working on a plan, discarding some ideas outright or refining other ideas until they too were discarded because of their impractical applications.

Bibi paused, stared at Olivia and said, "I know that."

This had been their third night in a row together, and their lack of progress frustrated both of them. Cracks were starting to show in their demeanour.

"Let's start at the beginning."

Bibi groaned.

"I know. I know. It might help. What do we want? This guy in jail, right? For a long time?"

"Forever."

"Sure. How do we do that? We can't plant evidence. We'd still need the police to have a reason to be on his property to find the planted evidence in the first place, and according to Davis, they don't have anything like that."

"What about another 911 call? Wouldn't they have to check again?"

"That's complicated. Whose phone do we use? Who do we register it to? Do we make someone up and report them missing and then dial 911? Too many moving parts, I think. If we do something, it has to work, because we won't get another chance."

Olivia's eyes glazed and she smiled.

"What?"

"I was thinking that could be the premise to a comedy. You know, trying to frame someone with elaborate schemes that fail in some comical way."

"Yeah. Hilarious." Bibi noticed Olivia's face fall and she said, "Sorry. My fault. This guy, he's messing with my head."

"I know what that's like."

"Probably better than me."

"Or maybe the same. Ever wonder if there is a limit to awfulness? To the feeling of it? That at some point, something can only be so terrible because we don't possess the faculty or equipment to process a super-awful experience? A pain threshold of a sort?"

"I don't know. Experiences are so personal. You think you can explain them to someone else, but there don't seem to be words for it. We can talk because you know what I mean when I say fear. You understand in a way no other friend of mine ever could."

"Yeah. We earned it."

"I guess we did."

The silence stretched out comfortably.

Olivia broke it first, she said, "You know, I feel gross saying this, but what we really need is bait."

Bibi mulled that over while chewing on a bail. Bibi said, "I think I got something. Yeah."

"Ok. What do you got?"

Bibi told her.

Olivia didn't like it. Not one bit. It was too simple. Bordering on stupid. They argued about it and Olivia understood later that what she thought was arguing had been a concerted effort to refine the plan until it became palatable. Olivia agreed because she understood they were going to have to lie to the police. In order to do that effectively, there had to be very little to lie about, very little to trip them up. In the end, Olivia agreed because they had nothing else viable to pursue, and in a simplistic way, it made sense. And it felt like they had no choice. The police couldn't stop him. Thinking about the killer and what he had done to Bibi and about the possibility of him holding people hostage right now for his own twisted amusement, Olivia felt, in this matter, she had no choice but to help. And using bait, well, if you wanted to catch a shark, you had to chum the water.

-46-
Education Part 12

Patience and self-control were the keys to his freedom. Patience when waiting for prey. Self-control in only taking prey that afforded the best possibility of success. He taught himself both, repeatedly reinforcing them over the years. Waiting in the forest, sometimes he'd go months without making a capture. He'd been tempted and every time he was able to suppress his urge, his need, to scoop someone when it appeared somewhat safe.

He learned camouflaging yourself to blend in with the ground was easier than attempting to fade into the background of trees or higher up in the branches. Evolution had taught people for millennia to recognize the shape of a human. More often than not, in ancient times, another human not of your tribe or group proved dangerous. The eye had a way of seeing the shape through the most elaborate disguise. The detriment to being on the ground was that it limited your field of view. Unless you had positioned yourself perfectly, blind spots abounded. He had learned that the hard way.

His positioning had been the problem although at the time he didn't see it. Flat to the earth, covered in leaves, debris, and dirt, he saw a lone person approaching on the path. A middle-aged woman, fit, carrying a large heavy backpack. The straps dug into her shoulders. Sweat darkened the red of her shirt between her breasts. Rucking, a newly popular form of fitness taken from the army training manual. Fill a backpack with something heavy and then go on a long walk. He thought of trying it out himself to see what all the fuss was about. In the moment, he saw perfect prey. Exhausted, she wouldn't have the energy to fight him off if he didn't get the initial ambush strike to take her out. He gripped the sap in his hand. He tensed his muscles. He studied the trail behind her and didn't see anyone.

He moved to the trail, studying the spot behind her ear that he'd strike, and then she stopped and turned back. He held still.

The woman said, "Are you all right?"

The killer didn't see anyone, but he heard the man reply, "No. But let's keep going anyway. I'll breathe later."

She smiled. The man stood. Overweight, sweating as though he'd fallen into a pool, with a large backpack strapped to him, the man stumbled forward.

The killer pressed himself flat to the ground. He hadn't seen the man. This could have gone terribly wrong. And it all came down to his positioning. If he hugged the ground to wait, he should be in an elevated spot to see the entire trail. He had missed the man because the man had been bent over, recovering from the exercise. The killer learned to scout his areas out ahead of time, before he set up, to find the perfect position. Patience and self-control will be what saves him. And like any skill, they needed to be constantly worked on.

•   •   •

Carmela and Ken became old news. The media had other fish to fry, other clickbait headlines to generate, usually containing dire information about COVID and how, because of variants, we may never be free of the virus and must prepare ourselves for a lifetime of mask-wearing and boosters.

With the news pushing those headlines, the police wouldn't be on his front step so often. He was certain they were keeping watch on him. To be safe, he hadn't left his property. He did clean out the crematorium, removing Carmela's ashes and sprinkled them over the grass of his property. He had done that at night, confident the police didn't have an infrared satellite pointed at him. And he tightened up his own home security.

Delving deep into the Canadian Criminal Code, the killer read about what was called a 'general warrant'. What did that mean? That meant if the police needed to use a new technique or tactic in gathering their evidence, they would write a general warrant. This included sneak and peek tactics. Theoretically, police could write a warrant, get it approved by a judge to sneak into his home, find evidence, and boom, he'd be in jail.

He wasn't truly worried about that happening. They'd never sneak in when he was home. He hadn't left his home for some time now and he didn't plan on doing so. Instead, he thought, as a precaution, he'd set up motion-sensor cameras on the property and in his home and in his garage, just in case.

If they got that close, it would be time for him to split. The project gave him something to do. He ordered the wireless cameras, extra batteries, and a burner phone to download the appropriate app to receive alerts and to watch it.

He didn't expect the police to get a warrant to search his home. He was confident they didn't have enough evidence to convince any judge to allow that. And the reason for his confidence was his continued freedom. This was more of an insurance installation. Because like insurance, it was better to have it and not need it than to need it and not have it, right? And if he had to leave, he'd feel safer returning knowing no one had snuck into his home. He never expected the police to appear in his home without his knowledge. If they came, it would be with a warrant to arrest him and search his home. Never in a million years did he expect to see Bibi's face floating on the screen of his phone. But he did.

-47-

Bibi and Olivia drove past Walt Griffin's place while maintaining the posted speed limit, trying not to draw attention to themselves. With the police surveillance finished, and the tracking warrant having expired, Olivia knew the OPP patrolled this area and it wouldn't do for Davis to learn she had been in the area by getting pulled over for speeding. As they passed, both heads craned to take in the home and the separate garage behind it. This was the fourth time in two weeks they had made the trip. The AC in the car blew cold air on both of them to combat the blistering summer heat. The lawn immediately surrounding Walt's home was kept short and well maintained. The rest of the field left unshorn, grew wild with yellow and purple flowers adding a pastoral element that could grace the canvass of an Emily Carr painting.

Bibi said, "It looks so... normal."

"Yeah."

The back windows of the car were open about three inches. It diminished the effectiveness of the AC but Freya and Odin liked the fresh air and had their snouts pressed to the gap, sniffing, their eyes closed in doggie ecstasy. Brutus stayed at home and Olivia couldn't help the twinge of guilt tweaking her now and then remembering the recrimination in his eyes while lying on his doggie bed as she closed the door. What they were planning to do Brutus wouldn't be able to participate in and in her mind, he had suffered enough. He was the last link she had with Harry and she wouldn't put him at risk for anything. On the other hand, she appeared fine with risking Bibi's life. A plan fraught with danger. A plan where too many things could go wrong and could mean the death of Bibi. And here she was, going along with it, because the idea of another Gorilla or Jackal running around, murdering people with the police helpless to stop, filled her with rage. Not an out-of-control-foaming-at-the-mouth rage. This was cold anger, as though her guts were bathed in liquid nitrogen. The objective, to catch

Walt Griffin, shone in her brain like neon. She would prefer to be the star of their script, but that wouldn't make sense and if they were to convince the police, their plot had to be realistic.

Olivia said, "When do you want to do this?"

"When it gets dark."

Did Bibi's voice quaver?

"You sure you want to do this?" Olivia asked.

"Yeah."

•   •   •

"You got everything?"

Bibi patted the knife on her hip. Touched her back pocket, felt the taser, and with her phone in her hand, she said, "Yeah."

"You have the burner phone?"

"Oh," she patted another pocket, felt the hard edge and said, "Yeah."

"Make sure you text me from that one before you call the police. They'll want to download the information from your personal phone for evidence later."

"I know. And I will make sure."

They were parked on tire ruts in the dirt, leading to a field of corn. Freya and Odin sat on either side of Olivia. Their eyes were locked on Bibi, Freya's head tilting as though questioning Bibi's sanity.

Olivia didn't know what to say. She shrugged, and said, "Good luck," knowing how lame the utterance sounded.

Bibi nodded, blew air out of her mouth, and said, "It's hot out."

"You're wearing a winter cap. It's the summer."

"It's dark."

"Your hair is dark. I don't think you need the cap."

"Yeah." Bibi took off the cap and tossed it onto the passenger seat.

Olivia said, "Stick to the plan."

"Yeah."

"You ready?"

"Yeah. Ok. Yeah. I'm ready. Let's do it now before I chicken out."

Olivia punched her in the nose and as Bibi staggered back, Olivia followed it up with a punch to her cheek.

•   •   •

The plan, if one could call it that, was simple. Sneak into the killer's home, garage, whatever, just get on the property and call the police, scream for help, drop the phone on the ground, leaving the line open, and hide until the police showed up. She'd have a swollen nose, with a bit of blood leakage to help sell their narrative. If all went well, Bibi would say she'd been kidnapped, and since she had been a previous victim, it would have a certain logic to it. To kill the only surviving witness as the police were closing in on him, would be a motive any prosecutor could sell. That was the plan as Olivia knew it. Bibi's plan entailed a different ending. Olivia had killed her Gorilla, her Jackal, and now Olivia was free. Free in a way Bibi was not even if she wouldn't admit it. As long as Walt Griffin lived and breathed, she'd never be free. Every shadow would assume a human shape. Every breeze would contain his voice. And no forest, woodland, would ever be the magical place she traversed before his wicked shape grew from the ground to take her. He had to die. His death would allow her to reclaim her life. It had been on pause for the past five years. It was time to hit the play button again.

•   •   •

Bibi entered the cornfield. The sounds of the outside world ceased to be. Her coat brushed the leaves drooping from the stalks, her shoes crunched on the hard dirt, and the noise of her breath leaving her mouth made the experience otherworldly, as though she'd stepped into another dimension. Through the stalks overhead she saw a part of the moon peeking out from behind a dark pillow of cloud. If cars passed on the road forty feet from her, she wouldn't know. The corn created a soundproof alley.

She took out her burner phone and glanced at the map. She had pinned the address on the map. A blue, blinking dot represented her on the map and a red pin represented her destination.

She and Olivia had talked about not engaging the madman. She was only to get on the property, call the police while screaming for help, and wait. Her injuries and her location would damn Walt Griffin once and for all. He'd be arrested and charged with kidnapping, and she'd be free. Bibi didn't buy the last part. Her freedom depended on Walt being dead. Olivia had killed her tormentors… both of them. And although Olivia hadn't completely healed, she walked around with confidence, knowing and believing the unlikelihood of another abduction by two masked men. Olivia could sleep at night. Bibi slept, sure, if you called two hours snatched here and there sleep. Walt Griffin, the huntsman, became the shadows in her room. The dark crack in an open closet. The hand waiting to grab her foot as she left the bed. The huntsman in prison wouldn't alleviate her fear. It wouldn't even put a band-aid on it. He had to die. And she hoped, hoped with all her heart, that Olivia would understand.

She stopped on the edge of the cornfield, hiding between the stalks. The house, his house, the monster's lair shone in the darkness. She exhaled. Sweat beaded her brow. Under her jacket, her shirt clung to her skin. Bibi crouched and crept forward.

•　　•　　•

Approaching the home, she repeated in her head her plan so often it became a mantra. Get to the garage, lure him out, hide, hit him with the taser, bury the knife in his chest, text Olivia. She shortened it and shortened it in her head until she reduced it to, garage, lure, hide, hit, bury, Olivia. She had to admit to herself the plan depended on a bit of luck and the belief that the killer would be too arrogant to lock up everything when he was on his home turf. Home was safe. And when you're one of the evilest bastards on the planet, you'd almost hope for some burglar to happen on your home, begging to be a victim. With that in mind, she hoped the side door to the garage door, not the big roll-up one, would be unlocked. She'd open the door, bang it back and forth a few times, trying to make it seem as if the wind had opened it, and wait. *What if he wasn't home?* That'd be terrible and, to be honest, almost a relief. Anyone else hearing her plan might think it needed work, some refinement, but she'd done her research. She was laying a trap. It's what serial killers did. Create a situation that on its face appears harmless, but needs to be addressed. Like an open door. Or a harmless man in a cast who needs help (Ted Bundy) or hitchhiking in a car with a university sticker on it from a local university (Ed Kemper). Innocuous circumstances that turned out to be deadly. Bibi was laying a serial killer trap for a serial killer. Bibi was the bitch Karma had been talking about. That didn't mean she wasn't terrified. With her back pressed to the side of the house, she peered around the corner expecting to see him there, waiting in the shadows for her. He wasn't. She measured the gap from the back of the house to the garage in her head. Forty feet? Fifty?

Crossing the gap would be the dangerous part. If he looked out a window, she had nowhere to hide. She almost quit right there. What a stupid plan. Leave the door open hoping he'll think the wind pried open the door? It wasn't even windy out. Not even a light breeze stirred the trees. She blinked and attempted to still the rapidly pounding drum in her chest. Go. Go and give it a try. If he doesn't come out, go with Olivia's plan. Call the police, scream, and wait for the damn cavalry and hope you can live with it.

Here we go. She stepped out from the house, patted the knife, touched the taser, and walked like a person crossing a pond on thin ice. Her head kept turning to the windows, expecting to see a man looking out at her and every time there wasn't, relief washed through her only to have the tension build again with the next step crunching on the gravel drive. *Why did she have to be so loud? Stupid gravel. Ever hear of pavement you psycho?*

She drew closer to the door. When she raised her hand to reach for the doorknob, her eyes widened, surprised. She felt no sensation of moving her arm or her hand. They acted on their own, disembodied, or at least it felt that way. Her gloved hand trembled as it made its way to the shiny silver knob. When the back door of the house boomed open, she full-bodied-flinched. Pounding steps on the gravel approached, she turned her head and body to face the threat but before she could complete the turn, he smashed into her, catapulting her into the steel garage door. She heard a 'klonk' and for a brief second pictured the word in cartoon letters ballooning above her head like she'd seen once on an old Batman show. She collapsed to the ground.

She couldn't see. She blinked, blinked, blinked and only saw a kaleidoscope of stars behind her eyes. Salty liquid in her mouth. She choked on it and it sprayed from her mouth in a mist.

Rough hands went through her pockets. He disarmed her, took everything, her items hitting the gravel with their weight, and she could do nothing about it. Her body wouldn't obey her commands.

She heard him say, "Two fucking phones again? Is this a new thing?"

Her vision cleared. Stars punctured the dark blanket of the sky.

He leaned over her. A crescent moon of white teeth shone from within the darkness of his beard.

He said, "Missed me?"

He punched her once, twice, three times and darkness.

-48-
EDUCATION PART 13

He had never been religious. In a moment of self-awareness, he questioned himself as to why he thought he was so right about there being no intelligent designer, no benevolent sentient being in the sky who cared for the little ants on this tiny planet amongst trillions of others. He did what he usually did when taken by a subject: he read. He read religious books (the Bible, Torah, Qu'ran, and others) religious philosophers (St. Thomas Aquinas, Isaac Newton and others), and the other side of the argument, he read books supporting the argument that God doesn't exist (Richard Dawkins, Christopher Hitchens and more).

In the end, he concluded religion held no answers for the meaning of life. The different religions fought over everything and since all of them believed their god was the one true god, no ground was ever given. This has always been the case. Even when the gods were plentiful and specialized (gods for fertility, gods for harvests, gods for war), everyone's god was the true god, the right god. The killer decided that your religious beliefs, more often than not, depended on geography, or more simply, where and who you were born to. If you were born in the west, chances were, you were told about Jesus from a young age. If you were born in the middle east, you worshipped Allah and Mohammed as the one true prophet. Depending on where you were born and whom you were born to largely determined what god you would believe in. It was not a truth a person arrived at on their own. They had to be nurtured into the belief from a young age by people they trusted, family and their religious community. If there was one true god, why all the confusion? If there was one truth, why were there so many versions of it? The killer believed that no one knew. To him, it made sense for early humanity to see religion as a way to explain the unexplainable and, in some way, hope to control the uncontrollable. Don't know what that streak of light crossing the night sky is? God did it and he's angry, better sacrifice a virgin. You want to make sure your harvest will be plentiful this season, so you don't starve? Pray to the right god and they'll help you out. With humanity's ever-increasing knowledge of the world around them, religion's cracks were showing. As Nietzsche had said, "God is dead. God remains dead. And we have killed him."

There is no meaning to life but what the individual gives it. There were no divine laws or a divine judge at the end of life. There was no one or entity that would send him to hell. He could do whatever he wanted; pursue any goal, and only other people could hold him accountable. But only if they caught him. The killer derived the meaning of his life by seeking the ultimate pleasure. The taking of human life, the accidental sentient ape. An Epicurean pleasure-seeking philosophy, except for the murdering part of course.

• • •

Before Bibi set off his motion-sensor cameras, the killer had been installing a chin-up bar in his basement. He wanted to add weight to a weight belt, to add intensity to his back workouts, and instead of doing bent-over rows all the time, he thought he'd spice it up with something different. After finishing drilling the holes in the studs, he picked up the chin-up bar and placed it where he had prepared it to go. He'd have to fold his legs back when doing the chin-ups otherwise his feet would hit the floor every time. His ceiling was too low. The garage might be a better place for his expanding gym. His phone buzzed in his pocket and brought him back to the now. Frowning, he plucked it from the back pocket of his jeans. Camera alarms. The cops? Blood rushed through him. A chill jellied his legs. He opened the app and no, it wasn't the police. Only one person. A woman. A woman sneaking onto his property? As she rounded the house, one camera caught her profile.

"Bibi?"

The killer knew it was summer, but right then, it sure as shit felt like Christmas.

• • •

Standing over the unconscious Bibi, the huntsman placed both phones in airplane mode and dropped them on the ground to crush them under his boot. He hesitated. The two phones were significant. He didn't know why, but although Carmela had two phones, that was the exception rather than the rule. Would he figure out the mystery of the two phones standing here? No. And it'd be better if the phones were rendered inoperable. He stomped on the phones and placed the cracked devices in his front pocket. He removed Bibi's coat. He examined the taser. Pressed the button on the side, saw two blue bolts crackle in the middle, smiled, and put it in his back pocket. The killer put the knife into his other back pocket. He rolled up the coat and dropped it on Bibi's stomach and scooped her up. Grateful for the return of an escaped catch, the killer still did not like the circumstances. Questions upon questions battered him. How did she know where he lived? Why would she come here? What were the two phones for? Were the police far behind? Were they involved in this?

Carrying Bibi in the dark, hoping he was going in the right direction, he dismissed police involvement. They would never involve a former abduction victim, hell, any civilian, in what could prove to be a very dangerous situation. Police services, like any government bureaucracy or private business for that matter, were ever-present and wary of one word: liability.

The police were not involved. Bibi came to his home, sneaking like a thief in the night, to do... what? And why did she have two phones?

He stopped, spun in a circle, and muttered, "Where's the goddamn hidey-hole?"

He shook his head. Should have brought a flashlight.

He put Bibi down, removed his phone from the only pocket not containing items taken from Bibi, and used the flashlight on his phone to scan the ground. There's the hill. The killer stepped toward the hill, wanting to open the door first and then come back for Bibi, but he remembered what she had done the last time he left her alone for a brief period. Her escape had him change how he dealt with all his prey.

He scooped her up and placed her down right by the door. He opened the door, threw the coat from on top of Bibi's stomach down the hole and picked up Bibi again, but this time, held her in a fireman's carry. He descended four steps, flicked the switch for the generator, and the hole brightened with incandescent light.

He carried Bibi to the chair and secured her. Because of his history with Bibi, he double-checked the straps. The killer touched her nose and one side of her face. He hadn't done that. He knew where to hit someone to knock them out. Now, it was different for everybody, the force of the impact and the exact spot was never quite the same, but they were similar. There are a bundle of nerves behind the ear, that when struck, can cause the brain to shut down. That's what made the sap effective. If delivered properly, the sap hit those nerves. He had aimed for that spot this time and had rendered an excellent strike. He hadn't hit her nose, so why was there blood there? Why was there swelling on the right side of her face? Those injuries hadn't been caused by him.

He closed his eyes picturing the moment of impact when he slammed into Bibi and she hit the garage door. Had her face hit the wall or door? No. The back of her head, her shoulder and part of her lower back had.

He opened his eyes and touched her nose. Who had done this?

This didn't feel right. Not at all. His stomach tightened and he backed away from Bibi, as though she was radioactive. Get back to the house and wait. Don't do anything until you understand this, whatever this is. Before he left, he stuffed a gag in Bibi's mouth and secured it there with a strap. He left his cave, turning off the lights and the generator as he went. She wouldn't need to see and why waste energy?

-49-

Olivia checked her phone again. No text from Bibi. She looked at her watch. Almost forty minutes have passed. Bibi was supposed to send a text once she was on the property and ready to start their dramatic enactment of an abduction. She should have been on the property in ten minutes. What was she doing? Olivia had sent a text fifteen minutes into her wait. No response. She considered calling and thought better of it because what if she was hiding? Would the buzzing phone give her away?

Olivia stood outside her car. Freya and Odin were sitting at heel on either side of her. She said, "What's she doing?"

Freya and Odin tilted their heads at her voice, their eyes studying her in the darkness.

Olivia, holding her phone at her waist, began pacing back and forth, staring at the screen, willing Bibi to text, to call, to anything. Forty-one minutes have passed.

"I'm going to have to do it. I can't wait any longer."

She ground her teeth, stared at her phone and said, "C'mon Bibi!"

Olivia had no choice.

She called Davis.

-50-

"You did what?"

Davis, at home, watching *Mindhunter* on Netflix with Sandra, had been enjoying the evening on the couch, beer in hand, watching Ed Kemper eloquently talking about his own motivation for murder. It was the first evening in a long time he'd spent with Sandra without thinking about Walt Griffin and who he might take next because the service didn't want to spend the money on surveillance. For once, an evening without anxiety. Until this late evening call from Olivia and the brief run-down of their absurd and dangerous plot.

"Goddamnit Olivia. I… just… stay where you are. Don't go near the home. I'll call in the cavalry."

He hung up on Olivia, called his Inspector, told her what was up, and she assured him uniform police and tactical officers would be on their way. She told him to call his team and head out to Walt Griffin's home with all haste.

After he got off the phone with his Inspector and members of his unit, Sandra, brow furrowed with a frown bracketing her lips, said, "What happened?"

He told her, as brief as he could while collecting his gear and when he had finished, Sandra said, "She did what?"

"I know. Look, I gotta go, and don't wait up."

"Yeah. Like I'll get any sleep."

"Sorry. I'll call when I know more."

-51-

Olivia heard the sirens, saw the rotating red/blue/white lights approaching and then passing her on the roadway, bringing dust and debris in their wake. She looked at her watch. One hour and six minutes had passed.

"What have we done?"

-52-
EDUCATION PART 14

There are no certainties in this world other than uncertainty. The only constant is change. When faced with uncertainty, it is almost always better to understand, as best you can, the situation you find yourself in before proceeding. Any action must be conducted in a position of near certainty. He learned that from his father. His father, as time went on, almost always operated in a state of uncertainty, paranoia and suspicion. It was that, more than anything, that unravelled his father's powerful intellect and, in the end, lead to his own demise. With the killer's help of course. What had he learned from that? Understanding should precede action. Blind action needs luck to succeed. Luck is a fickle mistress to appease and a concept he didn't believe in.

•   •   •

When the killer didn't understand a situation, it bothered him. An itch, teasing his cerebellum, poking, nudging and prodding him to resolve the enigma. How did Bibi know where he lived? Why did she come alone? She had two phones, a taser, and a knife. Had she come here to kill him? Again, why the two phones?

He would ask her, but he would wait. He wanted to make sure no one would be coming for her. It wouldn't do to be in his hidey-hole if someone showed up. He would know by way of his camera system, but it would be strategically beneficial to head off any rescue attempt and more importantly, to be aware of who was attempting to rescue her. He left Bibi in the dark and not because he wanted to add to her fear (although that was an added benefit). He didn't understand the Bibi situation. And he didn't think it prudent to interrogate her on the 'why' now when he didn't understand her purpose or know if anyone else was involved. He left, walked back to his home, made a coffee, picked up a book and read by the front window.

He heard the sirens first, then in the distance, the approaching lights. He exhaled and wondered if today would be his last day as a free man. They were coming to his home. They believed Bibi was here. And they were right. The only question was, how certain were they? This time, he wouldn't open the gate for them. They could park on the road.

•   •   •

The long line of uniformed officers hopped over the gate and approached the house. The killer opened the front door and leaned against the frame. He had exchanged his white shirt for a black one. Carrying Bibi through the hot summer air had made him sweat.

He said, "Back again?"

A tall officer in a grey tactical uniform said, "Yeah. We're going to have to search the grounds again."

"Can I ask why?"

"Detective Davis will be here shortly. He can explain everything."

"Ok then. Search away. Again."

-53-

Fifteen or so minutes after the first influx of officers, Davis and Stacy climbed over the fence and approached the house.

Stacy said, "Cameras."

Davis' eyes went to where Stacy had focused. On the corners of the house, he could see black fisheye lens cameras secured to the wall above window height.

"Those are new." *Had he seen Bibi approaching?*

"Or maybe we hadn't noticed them the first time."

"No. One of us would have noticed. They're new."

The front door opened before them. An officer in full tactical gear, helmet and goggles, nodded at them as they entered.

Davis said, "Find anything?"

"No. Not yet."

"What about the K9 dogs? Anything?"

"Still don't have anything. They're all up north again. Another meth lab project."

Davis said, "We really need more dogs."

To Stacy, Davis said, "Can we call a nearby police service? For their dog? If they have one working that is."

Stacy said, "We can try, but how long can we legally stay on this property for?"

"Try anyway. We can decide after we know if they are available. I don't think we'd be criticized too much considering the information we have."

"Ok."

Stacy stopped in the hallway and brought out her phone from her pocket. Davis saw Walt sitting in the kitchen with his back to Davis. Wearing a T-shirt this time, Davis observed the broad back and sloping shoulders. Not a man Davis would want to run into on a dark, wooded path. He reminded himself to stay calm. Dread pulsed like sludge through his veins. His chest felt constricted. Bibi was here. He had to get her back.

Davis stepped into the kitchen nodded at another officer in the room and she nodded back. Noticing the interaction, Walt turned and stared at Davis. Doll's eyes had more life to them.

Walt said, "I'm getting pretty tired of you being here detective. I'm considering a lawsuit."

"You're not the first person to say that to me. And I doubt you'll be the last. May I sit down?"

"No."

Davis pulled his phone out, to record the interaction, but Walt waved it away and said, "We're not doing that again. I'm done talking to you. Finish your search and get lost."

"You don't want to know why we're here?"

"Someone got lost again. And it would seem the place to start looking for every lost person is on my property. Once, again, search, find your nothing, and please, get out of here."

Davis handed his phone to the officer and said, "When I sit down, press the red button here. Try to keep both of us in the view."

Walt said, "I told you, I'm not talking to you."

Davis pulled out the chair, rubbed his eyes, and sat down.

"Don't talk to me. That's fine. I'm recording this interaction anyway. You know, to prevent any exaggerations for your lawsuit. And the cautions I read to you before, still apply. About calling a lawyer and all that? You want to exercise that right?"

Walt shook his head, said, "No."

"Now, I'm a cop. Have been for a long time. And although defence attorneys will argue otherwise, it's been my experience that there are no coincidences. Me being here twice, for missing people, is not a coincidence. *You* are the common denominator. You're a dangerous man. I've caught men like you before. The Jackal, for one. Hear of him?"

Walt smiled. The flint in his eyes didn't change, and it wasn't a smile of amusement. He said, "You didn't catch the Jackal. The girl did. Olivia wasn't it? You didn't catch anyone. How many people died before Olivia solved that problem for you? Her father was one of them, wasn't he? She seems to be better at your job than you are."

Davis reddened. *Stay calm.* He said, "You've been reading up on me?"

"You were in my house." As if that answered the question, and in a way, it did.

Walt continued, "You still talk to Olivia? I'd be surprised if she ever wanted to talk to you again. I do find it interesting that you tried to take credit for the Jackal. You should never utter falsehoods in an interview situation. I think it follows the same logic as attorneys never asking a question they don't already know the answer to. It can ruin your credibility. But you needn't worry. You had no credibility with me."

Davis breathed out through his nose. He did his best not to look at the officer recording. He knew she was staring at him. He had to turn this around.

"You got me. I didn't catch the Jackal. Wasn't even close. That Carl, an incredible actor when you think about it. How many people had he fooled over the years? Even his own family didn't know he was the Jackal. In any case, I wish everything had turned out differently. It's a case I will continue to think about forever and try not to make the same mistake twice." He paused, looked down in his lap and then raised his eyes, He said, "To be clear; I see you. I know what you are."

"And what am I?"

"I don't need to tell you what you already know. I'm here, really, to give you an out. I know Bibi is here. I'm not guessing. I know it. I know she came on your property. I know you found her. And I know you have her. I want you to let her go. I have a feeling she's alive, or maybe that's more of a hope, or an urge to not fail again, but either way, if she's alive and you let her go, right now, all your looking at is forcible confinement. Not abduction because you didn't take her and bring her here. She came to you. I know that. This time, you didn't bring it on yourself. What's the worst that can happen? You get arrested, sure, we'll do a warrant, and depending on what we find, there might be more charges or there might not. Either way, it's not a murder charge. It's not twenty-five years in prison. With the way the courts are going nowadays, with COVID especially, for forcible confinement, you might not even get jail time. I mean, they'd take your cooperation into account. Or at least your lawyer would make sure that the courts did. You should really think about it. Because if we find her first, all bets are off."

The small smile revealed in a creased cheek by his beard never left his face. The hard eyes examined Davis. Davis never felt so exposed before, as though

Walt could see under his skin, his muscle, his viscera and whatever he saw, didn't impress him.

Walt said, "I have no idea what you're talking about. But you know, what? I think this time I will call my lawyer. You've been here too long in my opinion, and I'm getting sick of looking at you."

●　　●　　●

There were no dogs available to assist with the search. They had to rely on boots on the ground. Officers with flashlights walked over the large property, searching through the home and the garage. There had been no hard drive storage for the cameras. They didn't record footage. Connected to WIFI, they seemed to operate more in the sense of an alarm system with eyes.

They had been on the property for close to three hours. They were running out of time. Stacy thought they were pushing their luck every minute longer they stayed on the property. Davis' phone buzzed every few minutes from Olivia asking for updates. Every so often he'd reply with *Still looking*.

Stacy, as delicately as she could, enquired as to when they would leave the property. At what point did this become an illegal search? Has the emergent aspect of their search been spent? Davis struggled with leaving. What would happen to Bibi if they left? Was she even still alive? These questions would bring him back to the table with Walt. Those dark eyes, calling him out on his failure in the past, mocking him, letting him know he'd fail this time, too. There'd be another death on his hands, but this time, like with so many of Walt's victims, he may never get closure. And Walt would be free to do it again.

Davis' phone rang. He glanced at the display and answered it, "Inspector."

"Davis. Find anything?"

"No. Not yet."

"When are you thinking of calling it?"

"When we find her."

"Listen, his lawyer called our service lawyer and-"

"Inspector, she's here!"

"That might be true. Probably is true. You have to find her soon. Before midnight."

"What's going on? Why are you pushing?"

"Your guy there called a good lawyer from what I understand. An expensive, bossy one. Our police service lawyer, the one we have on retainer-"

"Grover."

"Yeah, that one, she sounded scared of this lawyer your guy called. Anyway, the impression I got is you've got to play this one real tight. The sooner you get off that property the better. Exigent circumstances don't last forever."

"She's here, Inspector. Bibi's here. We can't go. If she's alive right now, as soon as we leave, she's dead."

He heard the Inspector sigh on the other end. A pause ensued.

She said, "I'll leave it to you, then." What she meant was, *you're on your own.*

"I understand."

•　　•　　•

The Tactical team completed the search of the home and the entire lot, all the way to the treeline. They found nothing and had retreated to the fence nearest their cars. They stood, talking, impatiently waiting for Davis to call it off so they could leave. They all knew they had been here for too long.

Davis stood on the driveway. The summer air was redolent of dirt, trees, and his own sweat. Walt, framed in his front window, stared at him. Stacy stood to Davis' left.

Stacy said, "Are you sure she's here?"

"I told you what Olivia said. Bibi has to be here."

"Maybe she never made it onto the property. Maybe she chickened out. Stranger things have happened."

"She had two phones on her. Both of them haven't returned a ping. You think she turned off both phones before heading to this guy's house? A man she believed abducted her and was going to kill her? No way. Besides, even without that, because of him, because of our talk, I know she's here."

"How's that?"

"He never once asked how we knew she was here. He never once asked why we came onto his property again. Every person we interview always wants to know how the police came to be on their doorstep, or what evidence the police had to arrest them with so they could gauge, plan, exactly what to say or not say to us. But not that guy, Walt, or whoever he is. You know why that is, right?"

Stacy frowned, nodded, and said, "Because she's here. It didn't matter how we knew. It only mattered that we didn't find her."

Davis said, "That motherfucker. Look at him. She's here! I *can't* leave. We leave, she's dead."

"It's almost one in the morning. Over four hours searching a property without a warrant, boss, that's pushing it. We have to go. We have no choice."

Davis, more to himself than to Stacy, said, "He's right. I'm a failure. Couldn't catch a goddamn cold if I wanted to."

He turned his back on the house. Biting his lip, he dreaded telling Olivia what they hadn't found. Although, she probably already knew.

•   •   •

Davis walked Olivia through everything they had done, from when they noticed the new cameras on the house until the decision was made to exit the property without Bibi.

"You're leaving?" Her eyebrows climbed her forehead.

"We have to. We have no choice."

He had driven to her location, a short distance away, and told her face to face what the search had turned up, the lack of K9 support, and tried, as best as he could, to explain to her why they had to leave.

"I've got dogs. Why can't you use them?"

"A civilian trained dog led by a person who is emotionally involved in the case? That wouldn't fly at court."

"Court? What does court matter now? We need to save Bibi's life!"

"We can't go back there now. Exigent circumstances are gone."

"What good are you? What good are the police? What the hell is going on? What the actual fuck is going on here?" Her voice rose, incredulity mixing with anger. Freya and Odin stared at Davis. Freya issued a low growl.

"I know. I know how-"

"If you know, why are you leaving? She's right there!" She pointed over his shoulder at Walt's home, "He has her! What does it take for the police to do their jobs? I can't fucking believe this!"

She turned from him and paced in the dirt.

"Olivia-"

"Oh, wait, sorry, I can believe this! I mean, I should be the only person who could believe this keystone cop nonsense! I mean, I was a victim of it wasn't I? And who paid that price? Harry, that's who! We trusted you! I trusted you!"

She wouldn't look at him. Her eyes toured the ground around his feet. She was ashamed of him. Her body language telegraphed it better than words ever could. A hole in his stomach opened up and swallowed his heart. Tears threatened. His hands shook. She was ashamed of him and he knew, in a large part, he had earned her shame. He stepped toward her, Odin growled, and he stopped. Tension thickened the air.

He lifted a hand, palm up, and still not looking at him, she waved it away. With a saddened dripping voice, Olivia said, "Get out of here. I don't want to see you. I don't want to talk to you. Not now. Maybe never."

"Olivia, don't say that, please-"

"Go!"

-54-

Bibi awoke in the dark, could smell the dampness and thought back to the hole in the earth she escaped into all those years ago. Fabric stuck to her tongue. She pushed at it, felt resistance, and pictured a strap holding it in place. Like the one she felt across her forehead. The rush of blood flow excited by her fear aggressively pulsed into her injuries, causing the pain to flare. She pulled air into her nose, but she couldn't get enough, and in the darkness, yellow motes crowded her vision. The fear of passing out, and her concentrating on eliminating that fear, slowed her breath, slowed her heart, but didn't kill her imagination. He could be in here with her right now.

She thought of *Silence of the Lambs* when Clarice, stuck in the basement, in the dark with the killer, had no idea he pursued her wearing night-vision goggles. The image solidified and not only did it seem possible, in her mind, it became probable. He could be two feet in front of her, watching her widening eyes, flaring nostrils, and the tiny droplets of sweat merging with other tear-shaped drops before gathering enough weight to spill down her face.

She held her breath, wondering if she'd be able to hear him breathe. She inhaled through her nose, thinking maybe she could smell him. She detected only her own scent, her own ragged breath through her nose. Her body tensed against the straps, waiting for the killer to touch her, or to utter dark words.

When the door creaked open, she uttered a short scream behind her gag. Dirt tumbled on wooden steps. She didn't see anything until the generator purred to a start and the lights turned on, little haloes of light suspended on chains from a wooden, steel and dirt ceiling. She couldn't turn her head to take in Walt. She heard his boots clomp on the steps and she heard the creaking hinges, falling dirt, as he closed the door behind him. She heard his boots on the hard-packed floor. He stepped in front of her.

A smile appeared in the beard. He said, "The one that got away."

He turned his head, nodded, and stepped away from her. He returned with a chair. He turned it backward and sat on it, putting his forearms on the back, and leaned his chin on his arms. His dark eyes studied Bibi.

"Why are you here? And who did that to your face? Your friends in blue left an hour ago, and I'm wondering, how did they know you were here?"

He squinted at her. He said, "I'm guessing you hurt yourself, planned to call the police from my place and have me arrested for abduction. That's my best guess. But why the two phones? I don't get it."

He stood, put the chair back and returned to stand in front of her and crossed his arms.

"The question is, what am I going to do to you? I don't want to mess up this second chance you've given me, but I need to get you into that incinerator before the cops return."

He walked behind her. She heard the clink of metal. Tools, bolts, items being shuffled about. He stood in front of her. In his right hand, he held a yellow gun of a sort. Bibi read on the side of the contraption BOSTITCH. A black rail ran down the front of the tool. A nail gun. He held a nail gun in his hand, measuring her. He shook his head and returned the tool. More tools clanged and shelves rolled open.

Behind her, he said, "I have a lot of questions for you and no time to ask them."

In front of her again, he held up a yellow handled box-cutter.

"I'm just going to keep it simple. Cut your throat, burn you out of existence, and go on with my life."

He slid the blade out, focused on her eyes, and smiled. "Yeah. That'll work. I'm going to put on a splash suit first. Don't want your blood all over my clean clothes."

Her mind split into two halves. One half-watched the killer's movements, knew what they portended, yet remained detached. Like watching a movie or TV show, following the characters, but not caring too much about what happens to them. The other half of her was very much involved in her own circumstances. She smelled everything; her own sweat, the earth, the wood of her hard, unyielding chair, even the leather strap securing her forehead and the gag in her mouth. Hyperaware, this half felt the blood moving through her body, the sweat running down her face, and the stickiness of her clothes clinging to her skin. She struggled against the straps, her muscles aching with the strain. The uselessness of her actions foretelling the rapidly approaching end of her life.

He walked toward a metal closet in her peripheral. He opened it. The metal cabinet held white, full-body suits on hangers. Bibi wondered how many people he killed in this pit since he needed a whole closet full of these 'splash' suits.

She watched him select one and remove it from a hanger. He knelt down and untied the laces of his boots. Bibi guessed she had maybe a minute or two left to live. Tears obscured her vision.

-55-

Davis left and all the police left with him. A hole ached within Olivia's chest. She paced in front of her car, muttering to herself, tapping the knife on her hip, and thought through the options before her. Was Bibi alive? From what Davis said, they didn't know because they found no trace of her. That didn't mean much to Olivia. The police had proven to her to be almost useless. They didn't find Carmela, and they hadn't found Bibi. And did he even kill those he caught right away? Did he maybe hold onto them for a bit like the Jackal and Gorilla had?

Images of the pink room rolled across her vision. The Gorilla taking her while the Jackal leaned against the wall watching. She smelled him again. Heard the Gorilla grunt. Odin whined and Olivia shook her head as though to dislodge the images from her mind. She hadn't experienced an episode of such intensity for a long time. She tasted blood. Olivia had bitten her lip. It stung. Was the man, this Walt, doing to Bibi what the Gorilla had done to her right now? The police had left. What would stop him from doing anything he wanted? More importantly, did Olivia intend to do anything about it?

What if he caught me, too?

She stopped pacing. A vein throbbed at her temple.

What room would he have waiting for me?

To believe Bibi was dead would relieve the pressure on her to do something. You can't save a corpse. And in trying to do so, she may become the next captive. Olivia needed to be realistic here. What value would Bibi have alive when the cops were on the property searching for her? She'd have to be well hidden and made silent. And what is the best way to silence someone? You kill them. A smart killer would do that. And by all accounts, this man was smart. The police knew he was a killer and could do nothing about it. That took a person of intelligence. An intelligent person wouldn't keep a person alive when killing them was the safer route. Dead people make terrible witnesses.

Olivia could go home, satisfied she had done all she could for Bibi, and that their plan had been a foolish one. Olivia would be sad for a time. Sure. That's to be expected. But, (and here's the crucial part here, the real selling point of leaving) she'd be alive.

Olivia opened the back door of her car, pointed inside and Freya and Odin jumped into the back. She slid into the driver's seat, turned on the ignition, glanced in the rear-view mirror at her dogs and said, "Ready?"

As she turned her gaze forward, she caught the reflection of her eyes in the mirror. She was crying and hadn't realized it.

Olivia turned off the dirt driveway and merged onto the road. A short distance later she passed a house with the lights on in the front windows. Behind the home and separate from it stood a garage. The moment she could no longer see the lights behind her, she pulled over on the side of the road, parked the car, and exhaled. She turned off the car, picked up Bibi's cap from the passenger seat, and exited the car. She opened the back door, made a motion with her hand and Freya and Odin brought dust up from the gravel under their paws. They sat before her awaiting orders like two furry soldiers.

"We going to do this?"

Their ears turned forward to catch her voice like the old satellites receiving TV signals.

"Ok. Yeah. Damnit!"

Olivia's breath increased with rapidity. Her heart moved about in her chest as though untethered, like a rogue pinball. She couldn't get caught again. She couldn't be put in a room again, to be used and abused like some private toy for demented men, where body parts were snipped off, cut off or sliced off with a razor. She could end up in that situation again. And for what? For someone who, if we're talking probabilities here, no longer wandered through the land of the living. *Not someone, Bibi, you're talking about Bibi here…*

Every so often, Olivia suffered panic attacks. They were less frequent as time from the events from five years ago stretched away. But in times of stress, unless she prepared her mind for it, her control melted. She clenched Bibi's hat in her hand and moved from foot to foot like a toddler avoiding the toilet. Harry had called it that, she remembered. He used to tell her of her toddler dance with a smile playing at the corners of his mouth. He loved telling her that. And she loved him too much to ruin the moment for him and say, 'Yeah dad, I've heard that one before, like a thousand times,' because to tell the truth, she loved the story too. Thinking of Harry, the good times, softened her breath and calmed her heart. She couldn't be caught again. And she couldn't leave Bibi to such a fate. Which decision would be easier to live with?

"Let's go."

She walked back toward the killer's house and brought her friends with her.

• • •

When Davis explained to her the police were leaving without having found Bibi, her anger precluded her from paying attention to everything he said. She heard him, understood him, but she didn't care what he had to say after he told her the police were abandoning Bibi. She ran through the conversation again because she remembered him talking about the home, the garage and the search. She and Bibi had looked at Google Maps before beginning their failed mission and understood where the house sat in relation to the open field and the trees that encroached on and bordered the land. What she had glossed over in the initial conversation with Davis were the cameras he had mentioned. The new cameras, according to him, were placed on the corners of the home. The killer had taken Bibi. She knew that for sure. The cameras had to have alerted him to a trespasser. To her, that meant they were motion sensor activated and would send an alert to whoever owned the cameras. She had security cameras in her own home. They were connected to her phone, and she could see in real-time, who was at her home. Since COVID, her phone had been lit up by notifications of delivery drivers dropping off packages at her door. Knowing that she couldn't directly approach the house presented her with a problem.

The cameras would be positioned on the home. Of course, they'd be. Where else would he post them? There were no poles or posts in the middle of the surrounding field, barren of crops and trees. What trees there were bordered the property, far away from the home. If cameras were placed on the bordering trees, not only would they have to have exceptional zoom capabilities, but they would also need either night-vision or infrared filters for the night to not render them useless. She knew such cameras existed and knew how expensive they could be. She had researched them herself for her own home, and based on that, concluded that cameras on the bordering trees would be impractical and cost-prohibitive. Yeah, it was a guess, but she was rolling with it. Conclusion: stay away from the home and all would be well. That strategy did present another problem.

How could Freya and Odin be expected to pick up Bibi's scent if she couldn't go near the home? Bibi had most likely been taken near the madman's home. And now, since the police didn't find Bibi or Carmela, Olivia believed Bibi was probably hidden away in a secret room, behind a secret wall. Secrets within secrets.

She hoped, she herself, would remain a secret from the killer. She hoped Bibi hadn't said anything about her. Hoped the killer hadn't read anything on Bibi's phones before destroying them. Had he destroyed them though? If Davis couldn't ping the phones to get Bibi's position, the phones had either been destroyed or turned off, or put in airplane mode. The question was, would he turn them on again to snoop? It would be risky to the point of stupidity to turn the phones on after escaping the police's handcuffs after two separate abductions.

Which brought her to another point. How had he gotten away with it twice? How was that possible? It was only possible if the killer had a hideaway. There must be one. And since the police couldn't find it, was the hidden room even in the house or garage at all? Why did it have to be? The killer had plenty of land to use for whatever purpose he designed. It was clear the man had developed an expertise in camouflaging himself. Why couldn't he transfer those acquired skills to camouflaging an entire room?

Freya and Odin were trained and exercised (by her) to track items. She never envisioned a situation in which she would need to use her dogs for such a purpose. She trained consistently, regularly, because the exercises provided structure and further cemented their bonding. It was a bonus that she had fun training with them. She had learned and continued to learn about animal behaviour and body language. They were never a finished product and she found herself looking forward to the next session, planning it out, to make it new and fun for all of them. Olivia wanted them to always obey her. They were her best friends and her trained protective service. She would now be putting all her training to the ultimate test. A real life and death situation. Had all her work been for nothing? A joke? Something to pass the time and humour a disfigured and sometimes lonely woman? The police couldn't find Bibi. What made her think she could? *Because I have no choice.*

How to succeed where the police failed twice? True, they didn't have dogs to aid them but when it came to finding someone who may or may not be in danger, they tended to overdo their searching rather than underdoing it. Why again, did she think she'd succeed when they couldn't? *Because Bibi is counting on me. And if I were her, I wouldn't want anyone to quit looking.*

Olivia had to succeed. And she had her dogs to help her. She would do what the police hadn't done. With her dogs, she'd start on the outskirts and work her way toward the home and garage.

Olivia clenched her hands around Bibi's hat. Ahead, the dark shadows of the treeline beckoned. A light breeze lifted loose bangs from her forehead and swayed the tall wild grass. The moonlight gave a white outline to the landscape. She marched forward. Freya and Odin, silent, kept pace with her by her side.

• • •

Olivia held Bibi's hat in her outstretched hand.

"Track."

The word's effect on Freya and Odin was immediate. Their bodies tensed, their ears turned forward, erect, like sails unfurling before the wind. Their snouts touched the hat, making chuffing noises, as they pushed the hat with their noses, taking everything in and storing it so they could find the smell out in the world and follow it.

Olivia pulled the hat back and said, "Track." She waved her hand away from her and said, "Go."

Freya and Odin separated, heads turning away from each other, their shiny noses turning to the light breeze. They moved as one, noses angled to toward the earth, their bodies squatting over the uneven ground, slunk in the same direction, tails intermittently swishing the air.

Olivia studied their movements and body language, and she smiled. She could tell they had detected something interesting. Hopefully, it was Bibi's scent they detected. Hopefully, they would lead her to her friend: alive.

Efficient furry machines. Olivia marvelled at them even though their effectiveness was directly attributed to the enormous time and effort she had put into training them. She was like a programmer, running and testing the software she created for this purpose. Unlike an unfeeling program, these animals, her family, her friends, loved to work, were excited to work because to them, this was their playtime. The dogs stopped, bodies taut as steel wire.

Olivia rubbed her arms. Goosebumps sprouted.

Both dogs, noses pressed into the earth, began moving in a zigzagging but purposeful way and then continued toward the garage over summer baked dirt and patches of starved grass amidst wavering tall grass. The closer to the structures they moved, their risk of being detected grew exponentially. Maybe the cameras on the structures did have night vision capabilities, not like they'd need them on a bright night such as tonight. Maybe the cameras' field of view extended right out to the treeline, further than she thought necessary, because what did she know? She wasn't a psycho-killer who liked to dress up as flora so she could nab anyone passing by. Still, she knew psychos. Had spent five years with two of them. That still didn't mean she knew this creep. She didn't know his mind. In this type of situation, not knowing could prove fatal.

She needn't have worried.

Freya and Odin stopped short of the house.

They pointed their snouts up, inhaling the night, trying to learn its secrets. Circling, stopping, scenting, and seeking upon a mound. A hill, but not quite. Not a hill to sled down in the winter, it possessed a gentle incline, rising to a peak of four feet higher than where she now stood. Freya whined. Odin pressed his nose to the earth, exhaled sharply, scratched at the dirt, paused and sniffed at the area he revealed again.

What had they found? A grave? Bibi's final resting place?

The muscles in her stomach tightened. She ground her teeth together. A chill violently shook her body. Was she doing this? Was she going to go through some shit again? Why was fate fucking with her so much?

Olivia walked up the incline, her hand tapping the knife always on her hip, ready for use, a talisman against the terrors of the world.

She stopped before Odin, where he continued to scratch at the dirt. She knelt before him, reached down and swiped at the dirt and grass. A hard, smooth, cool surface met her probing fingers.

A grave. A coffin covered with soil and grass.

Olivia said, "Quiet. Wait."

The dogs sat, watching her.

Using her hands, she investigated the dimensions of the hard surface under the dirt, wanting to find the edge of what she believed to be Bibi's grave. Instead, her hand found a chain. She frowned, climbed the links with her fingers until they ended at a round metal knob. She pulled on the chain. The earth moved under her knees, and she realized her own weight prevented whatever was underneath her from rising. Holding onto the chain, she moved away as far as she could without losing hold of the knob and pulled. Hinges groaned, the chain taughtened, and seemingly like magic, a hole appeared in the earth. When the door, or whatever it was, it had to be a door, opened enough, Freya and Odin darted into the darkness. Then they started barking. Angry barking, loud and echoing, their noise raised the hairs all over her body. With the ground door open all the way and against its hinges, Olivia let go of the knob. Moonlight illuminated the steps at the top in silver. Peering into the depths, steps at the bottom were lit by soft yellow light. Artificial light. An underground den. The monster's lair.

Mouth dry, knife now in hand, she navigated the steps on rubbery legs.

-56-

Bibi couldn't move her head. The straps held her firmly in place. When the sound of squealing hinges reached her, only her eyes moved to where the sound had issued.

The killer, her own private monster, had the white suit up to his waist and he was putting his arms into the sleeves. He paused at the sound of the hinges, surprise moving his eyebrows up his forehead followed by the tenseness caused by fear tightening his eyes.

Two furry blurs flashed past Bibi. They stopped in front of the killer, legs braced, backs arched, hairs ridged along their spines, tails bushed out, barking, angry, and spitting saliva out with every angry exhortation.

Olivia stepped into the light. Bibi's eyes moved to her. Olivia held her knife out in front of her, taking in the scenery with widened eyes and Bibi thought, there was anger in that gaze. More anger than fear.

Olivia said, "Quiet!"

Freya and Odin stopped barking. They bared their teeth and low growls escaped from their throats. The menace projected at the killer was palpable.

Olivia said, "One word from me and they'll tear you apart. So don't-fucking-move! Understand?"

The man nodded.

With her eyes on the man, Olivia hurried to Bibi. Being careful not to cut her friend, she sliced through the bindings holding her. It surprised Bibi to see the shine of tears on Olivia's cheeks. When did that happen?

Bibi stood; legs shaky as a newborn fawn. She blinked a few times to clear the stars from her vision. The straps had bit into her skin and her head and body still throbbed from when the man had slammed against her and then hit the garage.

She gathered saliva in her mouth, the gag had dried it out, and with effort, said, "Where are the cops?"

"They left."

"You came for me by yourself?"

Olivia nodded.

Bibi glared at the killer frozen by the threat the dogs represented. The white suit he was putting on still hung halfway on his frame. The suit he planned to use to kill her in. He didn't want to get her blood on his clothes.

Olivia said to the man, "Get down on your stomach. Turn your ugly head away from us and put your hands out where we can see them. Do it slowly. My dogs don't like fast movements."

His eyes moved to the dogs. They issued a loud growl, not liking the eye contact and the inherent challenge. He lifted his eyes and focussed them on Olivia. He said, "So, you're the second phone."

Keeping his eyes up, avoiding the dogs although it must have been a struggle, like not looking at a gun pointed at you, he lowered himself to one knee. His mouth set in a tight line, body thrumming with tension as though he expected those dripping fangs to sink into him within any second. Bibi watched him intently, knowing instinctively, like any fan of horror films, this would be the moment for him to try something. She saw his eyes slide to the knife he had dropped earlier to put on the suit.

Bibi said, "Hold it." To Olivia, "Let me grab that knife before he lies on it."

Olivia nodded, and said to the killer, "You better keep real still, now."

Bibi crept forward, body sore and tense, her injuries throbbing in sync with her increased heart rate. She squatted a foot away from the knife, half expecting the man to lunge for it or her. He didn't. Instead, his right arm reached behind him. The dogs growled.

Olivia said, "Don't!"

Time slowed and sped up at the same time. Bibi saw his hand come back in front with her taser in his hand. Olivia said, "Attack!"

Freya and Odin lunged for him. The killer stood, put his left arm in front and Odin clamped onto his exposed forearm. The killer grimaced but didn't make a sound. The taser in his hand zapped Freya in the snout. She yelped, collapsed to the ground, legs twitching, fur straightened. Olivia screamed. Bibi picked up the knife. Odin growled and tugged at the killer's arm, almost pulling him off his feet but the killer was too strong, so strong, he widened his stance, grounded himself, and reached behind him again, twisting further for the next pocket. A knife appeared in his hand. Olivia jumped toward him, with her knife in hand. Bibi pushed off the ground with the knife she had picked up. The killer buried the knife in Odin's neck and ripped and twisted it. Odin whined but didn't relinquish his grip. Before the killer could pull the knife free, Olivia and Bibi were on him. Their arms blurred. Stab, slash, stab, slash. The killer tried to jump back but he was pressed against the incinerator and had nowhere to go. Odin's blood showered the ground. Strength leaving him with the blood, he let go of the killer and dropped to the ground. Olivia and Bibi, screaming, continued to stab and slash. The killer fell to his knees, arms up in front of him. Olivia drove the knife down, sinking it into where his neck met his trapezoid. She couldn't pull it out, so she left it there, exhausted. The killer fell onto his side, still breathing, his body bleeding from multiple wounds, his flesh rendered to ribbons. Bibi, breathing hard, stood, staring down at the man who had been in her nightmares for five years. She heard Olivia crying.

Bibi turned her head. Olivia sat, with Odin's head cradled in her lap, saying to him through a voice choked with tears, "I'm sorry, I'm so sorry."

Odin licked her hand once before he stopped breathing.

•　　•　　•

Time passed. Bibi didn't know how long, but it felt like forever as she watched Olivia and then Freya mourn the death of Odin. When Freya recovered from the taser, she nudged Odin with her nose, smelled him, licked him and then issued one long howl. Olivia cried harder when that happened.

With Odin still cradled in her lap, Olivia said, "Is he still alive?"

"He's breathing."

The killer's eyes were closed. His chest rose and fell so slowly you had to watch for a time to see it.

Olivia said, "Help me get him in there."

"Where?"

"That tube there. That's an incinerator. It must be how he got rid of the bodies. I want to burn him while he's still alive."

The hairs climbed Bibi's arms. Olivia's voice was devoid of all warmth. Here was the woman who had killed two serial killers on her own. And now she would add a third.

The killer was heavy. Slippery with blood. Freya sat by Odin watching them. They put his legs in first and then with much grunting and slipping, they got him onto the table and pushed him inside.

Olivia slapped his face. Bibi didn't expect that, and she jumped. The killer blinked and Olivia slapped him again. His eyes opened. They found Olivia. He blinked. His mouth opened. Blood spilled from it.

Olivia said, "Fuck you."

Olivia started the incinerator and closed the door. She stood there until his screaming stopped.

•　　•　　•

Olivia said, "You never planned on catching him, did you? You wanted that to happen. You wanted to kill him, didn't you?"

"You killed your Jackal. I had to kill mine."

Olivia turned to look at Odin lying in his own blood. Olivia's eyes found Bibi. The anger in her gaze forced Bibi to take a step back.

Olivia said, "But at what cost? I'll never forgive you for this."

-57-

Davis hadn't slept since leaving Olivia and arriving home. He had always believed himself to be a good officer. He adhered to the Charter, followed the rules, did what he was supposed to do within the confines of the law. That hadn't helped him this time. It did the opposite, really. He knew Bibi was there. He knew Walt Griffin, or whoever he was, had her. His body language, his arrogance, confirmed his guilt in Davis' mind. Was that evidence? No. As police, it was their duty to preserve and protect life and he had left Bibi in the hands of a killer. He had failed. Failed in the worst way. He knew that. Olivia's horrified expression when she realized the extent of his failure, his gross ineptitude, had hammered the realization into him like a wooden stake through the heart.

No one could console him. Not Sandra. Not his colleagues. No one.

The pain was his alone.

In his mind, he had effectively killed Bibi. And Walt was free to kill again. Could he have failed any harder?

Once he returned home, Davis sat in his recliner, in his living room, the TV relaying more COVID news, the rise of cases and the deaths. None of the noise or sights registered. As irrelevant as the droning of insects.

Bibi's face. Olivia's condemnation. A continuous inescapable visual loop.

Sunlight slowly brightened the room. Sandra, on her way to work, told him she loved him, hugged him and said goodbye. He proffered a less than convincing reassuring smile. She left with a frown creasing the spot between her eyes and a promise to call him later.

What would happen when the press got wind of this?

He would be vilified, and he knew he had earned that vilification. Oh, there certainly was plenty of blame to hand around, spreading from person to person, touching some and ignoring others, as political blame tended to do. From Davis' experience, the lower you were in the hierarchy, more of the blame settled on you. Logically, the higher you were, the more responsibility you should have. That's what, for the most part, justified the higher pay. In real life, it didn't work that way. People were promoted, were paid more for less work and less responsibility. In the end, all fingers would be pointed at him. Having seen Machiavellian politics before, he used to get mad and defensive on a perceived victim's behalf. This time, he welcomed the blame and even the negative repercussions. He had killed Bibi. And he needed to be punished.

Davis hadn't eaten since the previous evening. Hunger tapped him on the shoulder, but he ignored the signals. After Sandra left, he didn't know how long after, his phone started to ring. He put it on the side table, by his hand, when he sat down hours ago. He glanced at the screen, not Olivia, an unknown number, so he ignored it. Unknown numbers usually meant someone from work calling. He didn't want to hear from work. Not yet. He didn't know what to think about the whole situation. He tried to process it in bite-sized chunks only the ideas, the images, collided with each other, refusing to resolve into a cohesive narrative.

The sun climbed higher into the sky. The bright burning bulb made him squint. He could have stood and closed the blinds. He didn't. The very idea exhausted him.

Then came the knocking at his front door. The insistent raps annoyed him. They were harder to ignore, and the courtesy bred into him caused him to feel a bit rude if he continued to ignore the knocks. He didn't want to see anyone. He wanted the world to fade away. He was grieving. For Bibi. For his lost friendship with Olivia, and the loss of faith in himself and his own capabilities. For his inability to do the right thing, despite the Charter.

The right thing wasn't always clear to see, though. It was shrouded in grey, cloaked in nuance and mystery. It hadn't always felt that way to Davis. He believed in the Charter, believed in people's freedom and had faith that if he followed the rules, everything would be fine. Except that was a lie. Bibi wasn't fine. Bibi was dead. He couldn't stop it from happening and for him, nothing would be fine again.

The knocking continued. His phone trilled and buzzed beside him. It must be someone from work, wanting to check on him. To make sure he still walked among the land of the ok, the super-duper. And until they made sure, they wouldn't go away. Fuck.

Groaning, he stood. He swayed, dizzy from being motionless for so long and then moving.

The knocking echoed; the phone danced on the table.

"I'm coming! I'm coming! Relax!"

He walked down the hallway to the front door, unlocked the deadbolt and opened it.

Stacy and Cameron stood on his porch.

Startled by Davis' red-eyed, haggard appearance, Stacy asked, concerned, "Have you slept?"

"No."

Cameron said, "It's Bibi. She's home. She called us from her neighbour's phone."

"What? Bibi?"

"Yeah. She's fine... well, as fine as she could be, I guess."

Davis stepped toward them and said, "Let's go."

Stacy put a hand out, "Hold on. You need to get cleaned up a bit."

Davis scowled, "Come on! I need to see-"

"Uniform officers are there, to keep her safe, until we arrive. She's safe. You look like hell. A quick shower, maybe brush your teeth, what's that gonna hurt?"

Davis said, "Ok. Ok. Wait. Does Olivia know?"

Cameron said, "She should. She's there with her."

-58-

The killer's blood coated Olivia and Bibi. Their hair was clumpy and sticky with it. Their soiled clothes hardened and stiff. The light of the coming morning teased the horizon as they walked to Olivia's car. They hadn't spoken a word to each other. Olivia's brow creased with thought. The occasional tear slipped from her eye to disappear in Odin's fur. She was tired of losing loved ones. Tired of being used. Olivia was sick of it, to tell the truth. Her hate for Bibi stoked with every step. Olivia couldn't wait to be rid of her.

They walked through the high grass, staying wide of the home, conscious of the cameras. Olivia didn't know if they recorded or not and didn't want to take the chance. Olivia carried Odin all the while, Freya whining beside her. Bibi walked on the other side. Bibi offered to carry Odin and received such a look of hate from Olivia she recoiled. They left the kill-room, with the incinerator still running, not caring if the entire place burned to the ground.

At the car, Olivia placed Odin gently on the back seat. She turned to Bibi and said, "You lied to me. You used me. All this bullshit about being my friend."

"No. That's not bullshit. You are my friend."

"Friends don't lie to friends. Friends don't use their friends."

Bibi scowled, "Don't be naïve. Of course, friends use friends. How do people escape loneliness? Friends. How do people find support? Love? Compassion? Friends. People use people all the time. It's not always a bad thing."

"You got Odin killed."

Bibi rubbed her arms. She said, "I know. And I am sorry about that. You have to know I didn't plan it that way. But I had to kill that man! And I *know* you understand! You know what it's like. It felt like I couldn't breathe for so long. Knowing he was out there, knowing at any time he could turn his interest back onto me, I could never be free."

"I don't know what to think." But she did. In a way, she knew exactly what to think. How long had Bibi planned this? From the moment Bibi asked Davis if she could meet Olivia? Maybe. Olivia was thinking Bibi had known what she wanted to do all along because Bibi needed someone like her, a killer of killers, to help her get it done. Keeping those thoughts to herself, she said, "I don't know who you are."

"Yes, you do. I'm you and you are me. Answer honestly. If you knew who the Jackal was, and where he was, and the police weren't doing anything about him, what would you do?"

Olivia, thinking of Harry, thinking of Brutus, nodded. Olivia would have ended the Jackal if she could have before he got to her. Before he got to Harry. The thought also reinforced her belief that Bibi had been planning this long before she let on. Olivia didn't like being manipulated. Evil men had done that to her. She hadn't expected a fellow survivor of horror to do the same to her. Someone she considered a friend. Even now, admitting she would have killed the Jackal if given the chance, Olivia said, "Fuck."

Relief lightened Bibi's body. After a beat or two, she said, "Now what do we do?"

Olivia said, "I'm going home. I'm going to bury Odin in the backyard, so I can visit him every day. Then, I'll clean up, hug my remaining family and feed them."

"After that?"

Olivia rubbed her face with her hands. She said, "I don't know. We can't tell the police. We murdered him."

Bibi said, "Only you and I know that."

Olivia said, "You know, Davis said what made this guy so effective was no one knew if the victims were just missing people, victims of hiking misadventures, or murdered. His murder hole, the police didn't find it, and they were on the property twice. We could just walk away. We don't have to tell anyone he's dead, do we?"

Bibi frowned, nodded, and said, "No. But, we will have to tell them I'm alive."

"Yeah. That's going to be tricky. But luckily, Davis taught me well, even if he didn't mean to. This is going to be hard though."

"Has any of this been easy?"

Olivia exhaled and said, "Good point. So, we are going to lie, and the police are going to know it, and if we do it right, there's nothing they can do about it. Just so you know, after this, you and I are done."

Bibi's eyes shone. She nodded and said, "I know."

-59-

Davis called Sandra, told her the news, hopped into the shower and was out before any hint of steam could mar the bathroom mirror. He shaved, brushed his teeth and walked out the front door and hopped into the back of the detective car.

He said, "Let's go."

Cameron drove, Stacy rolled up her window. The wind would tangle her hair into an unmanageable mess and in this heat, the AC made the ride more comfortable.

Davis rubbed his eyes, pushed his hair back from his forehead and watched the scenery pass while a cold knot of nervous energy tickled his insides. Olivia would be at Bibi's. Nervous about it, and somewhat discomfited by the nervousness considering Olivia had been one of his best friends for the past five years, the cold knot spread. *Had been.* Her disgust with him wouldn't have faded with the return of her friend. He had not rescued Bibi. Until a few short hours ago, he had thought he had killed Bibi. How would she look at him now, when he entered the room to find out what happened? He had a general idea of what happened from the uniform officer at Bibi's home. She supplied a short statement including the mysterious answer as to how she got home, Bibi said, "I walked." No further answers were forthcoming. No more clarity provided other than those two words. He knew she had used a neighbour's phone to call the police and, he assumed, to call Olivia, but other than that, he knew next to nothing as to what had happened out at Walt's place. A *Tim Horton's* drive-thru order sign appeared before his eyes.

Davis said, "What are you doing?"

Cameron: "Getting a coffee?"

Stacy: "And maybe a cheese tea biscuit?"

"Jesus, guys. You're killing me here." They knew how anxious he was. They knew how distraught he had been last night. And here they were, stopping for coffee.

Cameron said, "You want a bean?"

But since they were already here, Davis said, "A medium, one cream, one sweetener and you know what? I'll take a biscuit too."

•　　•　　•

A uniform officer stood outside the door to Bibi's apartment. She saw Davis exit the elevator with a coffee in hand first, nodded and said, "No coffee for us lowly uniform officers? Typical."

"Did you leave yours in the car? Is it cold now? Is that the problem?"

She said, "Maybe."

Stacy and Cameron stepped into the light powder blue hallway, grey carpet, and bright lighting. They trailed behind Davis.

Davis said, "How are they?"

The uniform officer shrugged, said, "As good as you could be, I guess. The one, Bibi? She looks a little beat up, shaken, but other than that, she seemed ok. She declined an ambulance."

Davis winced, said, "Beat up?"

"Yeah. Swollen nose, bruising on her forehead, couple of scrapes."

"Huh."

Davis knocked on the door.

Olivia opened it.

Davis said, "Hey."

Olivia, with a flat gaze devoid of emotion said, "Hey back."

•　　•　　•

Bibi sat on a loveseat. A cup of steaming coffee sat on the table before her. She had wrapped herself in an afghan blanket. A tremor passed through her. The TV mounted on the wall tuned to the local news with talking silent heads with serious no-nonsense expressions. On mute, the closed caption function was engaged. White lettering against a black background scrolled along the bottom of the screen. Adjacent on both sides of a loveseat were two matching single chairs. Olivia seated herself beside Bibi. Olivia's expression still hadn't changed. Not a guarded look, more a projection of indifference, a nonchalance par excellence.

"May I have a seat?"

Bibi nodded, and Davis sat in a single chair closest to Bibi. Stacy took the other chair, and Cameron leaned against the wall.

Bibi noticed Cameron and said, "There are chairs in the kitchen just through the door. You can grab yourself one and bring it back."

Cameron said, "Thanks," and returned with a chair and sat on it.

Bibi's hands appeared from under the blanket. She reached for the steaming cup, picked it up, and after a sip, held it under her chin. Davis saw the injuries and immediately thought she'd been beat up or in a fight. The swelling of the nose had the look of an after-the-bar fight, an injury he'd seen too often when on the road in uniform and responding to those calls. Usually, the person who had lost the fight (a fight they had started) wanted to report an assault to get back at the person who had the gall to embarrass them in front of others. Bibi's eyes studied Davis. She did not possess the skill Olivia demonstrated with her stone face. If Davis had to guess, he would think Bibi to be a little afraid of him. That can't be right. Already, before any questions were asked, his detective sense started tingling.

Davis said, "I can't tell you how happy I am to see you. I uh, well, let's just say Olivia's phone call last night... was it really only last night? Feels like forever ago. I didn't know if I'd ever see you or hear from you again. I'm so very glad to see you." He paused, his eyes welled, shone and Bibi blinked, unsure what to make of the emotion.

Davis inhaled, said, "As police, we would like to know what happened, and should we be looking for Walt? Arresting him?"

Bibi shook her head.

"Before we go there, I would like to audio and video record your statement, to make it official. Our phones have the capability to do that, and Stacy here, she'll do the recording with her phone, and yeah, is that, would that be ok with you?"

Bibi's eyes shifted to Olivia. Olivia didn't return the look. She stared at Davis with all the emotion of a piece of wood. Bibi turned back to Davis and said, "Sure. That's ok."

Stacy brought her phone out, tapped on the screen, frowning, and after a minute said, "Ok, we're good to go when you're ready."

Davis said to Bibi, "You good?"

"Yup."

"Okay, you've heard this preamble before, but I have to say it every time and well, yeah. This statement is being video, and audio recorded. This statement is voluntary. We are in your home with your consent. Is that accurate?"

Bibi said, "Yeah."

"If at any time you don't want to continue with the statement, say so and we'll stop it. If at any time you don't want us in your home, you can revoke your consent and we will leave. Do you understand?"

"Yup."

"Do you wish to provide a statement to police?"

"Sure."

"Ok. Good. I know what Olivia told me, about the how and the why you ended up at Walt Griffin's place, and the plan. Could you please go through it now on video?"

"Yes." And Bibi told them the plan of sneaking onto the property and calling the police to get Walt arrested for abduction, a plan she and Olivia had concocted.

Davis said, "Can you tell me what happened when you got onto the property?"

Bibi glanced at Olivia again. And again, no response from Olivia. No nod. No returning glances. Nothing. That's the second time she did that? Why?

Bibi put her cup down on the table, drew her knees to her chest and wrapped the blanket tight around her body.

"It's kind of embarrassing."

"There's no reason to be embarrassed. About any of it."

"Well, ok, I uh walked through the cornfield, worried about the plan and scared about going onto that lunatic's property, a big mess of emotions you know? Then I started to get paranoid, yeah, I know, but even more paranoid, thinking did I have everything I needed? Did I forget something? I know I checked before leaving Olivia. I know I did, but what if, in all my nervousness, I thought I brought everything but didn't? I went through my coat pockets, looking for my phones, and I felt them, and pulled them out and was like phew, at least I didn't fuck that up." Bibi's eyes widened, remembering the camera and said, "Sorry. I said fuck."

Davis smiled, said, "That's fine. Please, keep going."

"Ok, so I had both phones out in my hands, and this is the embarrassing part, I uh, the ground was uneven, it was dark, and where the cornfield ends, there was this sudden dip, like, what do you call those man-made dips that move water?"

"A water channel?"

Bibi continued with her narrative, eyes downcast, studying the cup on the table. She no longer made eye contact with Davis or with anyone else in the room. She said, "Yeah. I think. Anyway, it was like the ground dropped away in the darkness. I fell and put my hands out to break my fall. The phones went flying and I headbutted a rock on the ground. And well, for a bit there, I was unconscious. I don't think for very long, but I felt like I lost time."

Davis said, "You fell? And knocked yourself out?"

Still studying the table Bibi said, "Yeah. I woke up, groggy and then when I remembered where I was and what I was doing, I panicked! I felt all along the grass for my phones and found them only they had fallen into the water at the bottom of the channel. There wasn't a lot of water. There hasn't been a good dose of rain for some time now, but there was enough to soak both my phones and neither one would turn on. The plan was f- uh, screwed now, and I went back the way I came from to find Olivia, but she had gone. I couldn't call her. I couldn't call anyone. Not an Uber. Not a cab. I had to walk home. And when I got here, I used my neighbour's phone to call Olivia. She told me how she freaked out and called you guys. She told me I should probably call you and let you know I was okay. And I am. Okay."

Davis couldn't help himself. He turned frowning eyes upon Stacy who returned his gaze with her own flat gaze of suspicion. He knew the look and knew it well and was reassured he wasn't the only one who thought Bibi's tale had more holes in it than a hockey net.

"To recap: you fell, hit your head, and when you woke up, your phones didn't work, and you walked home?"

"Yeah. That's why it took me so long to call you guys. It was a long walk. Like over five hours."

"Where are your phones?"

"I dropped them. When I realized they wouldn't work, I was confused and pissed so I dropped them and kept walking."

"You dropped your phones? Both of them?"

"Yeah. I know. It sounds stupid. But I wasn't thinking right. Hit my head and all."

"You got those injuries to your face when you fell?"

"Yeah."

"They weren't caused by anyone?"

"No."

Davis couldn't keep the disbelief from his voice when he was asking the questions. He kept thinking about how Bibi had glanced at Olivia from time to time. How Bibi, when she got to the ridiculous part of her story, couldn't meet Davis' eyes. Had they planned this? What had they done? Why was Bibi lying? Davis had no doubt. It wasn't even a good lie. It was almost insulting to know they thought he might buy the sack of falsities she was selling. Or maybe they didn't have time for anything more elaborate. Maybe it didn't matter what story they told him. From what he had here, he couldn't prove or disprove Bibi's story. Unless Olivia would let him look at her phone, to see what communications had passed between them and when. But of course, Olivia would have to do that voluntarily and he had a better chance of learning to spontaneously breathe underwater than that happening. He didn't like how this was going. He was being lied to. And it was so blatant, they had to know he knew they were lying.

Davis said, "I'm sure this has been explained to you before, but before we continue, I'm going to have to caution you. While the police are conducting a lawful investigation, you don't have to tell us anything. But what you do voluntarily tell us has to be the truth. You can't lie. That is a criminal offence. It's called Obstruct Justice. So, I'm sorry if this sounds harsh, but I'm going to have to ask you this: are you sure what you told me is the truth? You can change it now and no harm, no foul. You were scared, whatever, all I'm saying is, right now, I need to hear the truth. Lying to the police… you just can't. Can you tell me the truth now?"

Bibi raised her eyes. There was anger there. No more avoidance of Davis' eyes. She said, "That was the truth. All of it."

Davis said, "I don't believe you."

Bibi said, "Hey detective? I'm revoking my consent. Leave my home. And don't ever come back."

Stacy stopped the recording. She stood, Cameron stood, and Davis, jaw clenched, stood last.

He held his hands out and said, "Olivia. I can't believe that."

"Did she stutter?"

"What?"

"Did Bibi stutter?"

"No."

"Then why haven't you left yet?"

Davis' face flushed. He knew Olivia. He knew to survive what she had survived, there was a hardness to her, an unyielding in her spirit. He knew it intellectually, and now he experienced it personally. She was done with him. In her mind, he was already a memory.

Davis said, "Okay. I'm sorry. I'm going to miss our friendship. I wanted you to know that."

Olivia said, "I'm going to miss who I thought you were."

-50-

Walt Griffin was never heard from again. Davis made attempts to contact him by phone, by visiting and pressing a buzzer at the gate no one ever answered. It ate at him. What had happened out there? He knew Olivia and what she was capable of when her back was against a wall, he suspected, but could never verify. Bibi and Olivia covered up something. He had lost Olivia in this. She wouldn't return his calls or acknowledge the cards he'd sent her in the mail. Even so, he never lost interest in the mystery of Walt Griffin. From time to time, while working on a missing person's case, or a homicide, his thoughts would return to Walt Griffin, and it would provoke him to drive out to his place. He noticed the property's decay, and then the bank's foreclosure sign and notice of auction on the front lawn. Where had Walt gone? Davis suspected. But so what? No more people had gone missing in quite the same way since Walt's disappearance (kind of ironic, Davis mused), and in the end, that was a good thing? Wasn't it?

About the Author

A busy father of four, John Hunt is a published author who had not started writing until late 2009. Most of his writing is done during his spare time. His short stories have been published nine times. He works and lives in the city Guelph, Ontario, Canada with his family.

Note from the Author

Word-of-mouth is crucial for any author to succeed. If you enjoyed *Olivia*, please leave a review online—anywhere you are able. Even if it's just a sentence or two. It would make all the difference and would be very much appreciated.

Thanks!
John Hunt

We hope you enjoyed reading this title from:

www.blackrosewriting.com

Subscribe to our mailing list – *The Rosevine* – and receive **FREE** books, daily deals, and stay current with news about upcoming releases and our hottest authors.
Scan the QR code below to sign up.

Already a subscriber? Please accept a sincere thank you for being a fan of Black Rose Writing authors.

View other Black Rose Writing titles at
www.blackrosewriting.com/books and use promo code
PRINT to receive a **20% discount** when purchasing.

Printed in Great Britain
by Amazon